# The House on Butterfly Street

Also by Mhani Alaoui

*Dreams of Maryam Tair: Blue Boots and Orange Blossoms*

*Aya Dane*

# The House on Butterfly Street

Mhani Alaoui

Interlink Books

An imprint of Interlink Publishing Group, Inc.
Northampton, Massachusetts

First published in 2023 by

Interlink Books
An imprint of Interlink Publishing Group, Inc.
46 Crosby Street, Northampton, MA 01060
www.interlinkbooks.com

ISBN-13: 978-1-62371-727-8

Library of Congress Control Number: 2023941536
LC record available at: https://lccn.loc.gov/2023941536

Printed and bound in the United States of America

*In memory of Aïcha Chenna*
*nurse, social worker, women's rights advocate*

*For my kids: Elias, Nacer, Zeyd*

# Contents

# Part I

# 1
# Caretakers

*Present-day Casablanca, one morning in spring*

The caretakers of the house on Saint Barthelemy Street, in the rapidly modernizing residential neighborhood of Palmiers, had flung its large bay windows wide open, letting the city's grayness and harsh morning light in. The air around lay low and heavy. It hadn't rained in months, though the winter season had long passed.

It was Monday, cleaning day. Jeanne Ba and Amber Draa had pushed the furniture against the walls and secured the more delicate objects inside the cupboards. Despite the drought, they had been told to prepare great buckets of water and black soap to pour over the tile and marble floors. Wasting water was the ultimate luxury.

Jeanne, who was in her early twenties, was Senegalese. Her local employers called her Zahra because Jeanne was a foreign name, and Zahra, which means flower in Arabic, is a softer and cleaner name. Despite her young age, she was also in charge of Al, the teenage daughter of the house's owners, who drew strange and beautiful drawings, and was afflicted by a mysterious illness.

Amber's last name, Draa, was a made-up one, for no one, not even she, knew what her real last name was. An ancient woman, known as "Dada," she was in her seventies, or in her hundreds possibly. Not even the authorities, who had delivered her ID card, knew her real age. She was the daughter and granddaughter of slaves—of Dada Yacout, her mother, and Dada Yasmine, her grandmother.

She was the granddaughter, too, of the master of the house, Mohamed Raiss, now long dead, who had taken her grandmother repeatedly, and at whim.

Dada is the ancient name for an enslaved woman who raises generations of children in the house that holds and keeps her. Slavery in Morocco was abolished over a century ago, but the name Dada lingered on. Dada Amber, though a free woman, had spent her entire life in the service of one family, and choice wasn't a word she had much use for. Today, as she walked painfully across the floor, Amber was worried and angry. Fearful images of the outside world filled her mind. No one would guess, from her heavy legs and bent back, that she had once been strong and vibrant—if it weren't for the light that still shone in her gray eyes, behind her thick glasses.

*Where did Ghalia go? Where was that girl?* she wondered.

Ghalia, the young housemaid, had not shown up for work in over a month, though she had only asked for two unpaid weeks in order to handle some personal matters. Ghalia Ait Iddin was quiet and serious. She never strayed from the task at hand and always managed to be clean and dignified, a feat Amber respected.

There were other aspects of Ghalia that Amber was suspicious of. For one, Ghalia, as far as Amber was concerned, was a beautiful woman: she could even have been a very beautiful woman if it weren't for her skin, too dark, or her hair, too black and thick. Still, women who looked like Ghalia didn't usually work in houses—they tried their luck elsewhere. This fact bothered Amber: in her long experience, people were rarely what they seemed, and what they wanted you to believe. She watched her, and she may have seen things.

But Ghalia had eased her burden: she took care of everything, intelligently and diligently. Amber, for the first time since she was six years old, knew a semblance of rest.

She had tried calling her a few times, desperate not to lose one such as Ghalia—the hard-working one, "the precious one," as named by her maternal grandmother who, from the moment she laid eyes on her, had loved her more than she had loved any son or grandson. Amber, whose own name (a warm color, a soft, translucent gem) was one given to enslaved girls or to daughters of enslaved women back in the day, told Ghalia that her grandmother had named her well. For she was indeed precious, and Amber, who was not one to compliment others easily, would be lost without her.

Ghalia could only smile and kiss the old woman's hand. The memory of her grandmother holding her in her lap as she sat in front of the stone fire in her two-room home in the village of Taounate, on the edge of the desert and surrounded by the Atlas Mountains, was one that turned her tamarind-colored skin cold and her honey-imbued eyes dark. Her grandmother had died too soon, and had taken with her the purest, most tender love Ghalia had ever known or would ever know. The family never again returned to her grandmother's village and left the tiny home to return to the desert sands.

And when Amber asked her why a young woman who could read and write fluently, and seemed book-smart, would agree to be a maid—weren't there enough illiterate women in the country to do the dirty work, Ghalia held up her strong, clean hands.

"Don't we all need to make ends meet? There are many young women in my situation. It's just a job, just to make money while I get through school," she explained, stroking Amber's worn hands, for the old woman, despite her strangeness, touched her in deep and unfathomable ways.

*And to get away from home,* Ghalia added to herself. *Only for a couple of years...*

---

Amber, despite her age, and Jeanne worked equally hard, and soon the house was clean and in order. They couldn't, however, quite get rid of the cold, underlying smell that permeated the house on Saint Barthelemy Street.

# 2
## Unraveling

Later that morning, in the rectangular, loft-like living area of that same house on Saint Barthelemy Street, Nadine Alam sat quietly at the breakfast table looking out onto the dried-up garden that stretched squarely outside the bay windows. Sitting up straight, her perfectly painted nails played with the cold coffee cup in front of her. She was thin, and her blonde hair was tied in a neat ponytail. She had light green eyes and high cheekbones, a straight nose, and a large mouth that barely smiled anymore.

Although there once was life and vibrancy in Nadine Alam, she had become a shadow of her past self, akin to a porcelain doll. She had turned into one of those upper-class women who belonged to another time, another world; frail and fragile, unable to withstand hardships, be they terrible or slight. She felt trapped. And she despised herself for it.

Nadine was often quiet, in the way the house was quiet, always quiet, except when they had visitors, which rarely happened these days; or when the housekeepers were busy with the weekly cleaning of the house, and they would talk and laugh and fight among themselves, sharing the music from their phones as they worked. Or when her husband, with whom she barely exchanged a word anymore, turned up the music as loud as he could and got drunk. She was often quiet, speaking as little as possible, because she didn't have many people to talk to and, more importantly, because Al, her seventeen-year-old daughter, hadn't uttered a word for close to two years. How could she socialize and exchange light-hearted banter, when her own daughter, plagued by an undiagnosed illness, could not even speak?

⸱———⸱⸱⸱⸱⸱———⸱

When she and her husband were younger, their friends admired them as a couple. He was tall, dark, and broad-shouldered; she, soft-spoken, light-skinned, light-haired and elegant. They were an ideal representation of a man and a woman. But as years passed and tragedy settled at their gates, their friends whispered that a curse had fallen upon their house, and they barely came to see them. And that was fine with Nadine; though Kamal continued seeking company outside the house.

He once told her that life with her was as cold as a fridge abandoned on Arctic ice and that she wasn't like other women. There were nights when he didn't sleep in their bed but in the empty room next to theirs. It was a room that had always been empty. Except for that one time, three years ago, when Nadine painted the walls a soft gray and brought in a cradle, wooden toys, and baby clothes. Otherwise, it had remained vacant, a room enlivened only by an extinguished hope and a disquieting present. The only person who ever entered it was Kamal.

As the man who shared her bed and her life slowly became a stranger, Nadine did nothing to keep him close. She had a secret of her own: she was relieved. And the reason for her relief, which she never shared with anyone, was simple: it was his scent. At first, his scent was musky and elegant, a male scent, full of the promise of money and security. But as time passed, it had become strong and unbearable. It was everywhere, surrounding him, his clothes, his sheets, his pillow, his car. It was a scent that mixed cologne, sweat, and aftershave, all to excess. And below it, right underneath its surface, Nadine smelled something else: rot.

⁕

This particular morning, she sat quietly at the breakfast table and stared at the large, brown, stained envelope that lay on top of the daily mail. It had her name on it, *Nadine*. The handwriting was unfamiliar. Someone had left it at the front door that morning, and she had hesitated before opening it.

Finally, she tore it open. Inside was a newspaper, dated two weeks prior. It had been read many times, and held too tightly. Someone had drawn a red arrow though the front, across the middle pages, and all the way to the back page. There, the arrow stopped at a headline in the miscellaneous news, the section that dealt with matters relating to culture and society. An article had been circled, also in red.

*In the working-class district of Ben M'sik, a woman gave birth to a little boy. The mother is a single woman, and the child is born out of wedlock. No one knows who the father is, and he hasn't made himself known, either to marry the mother or to declare the child, in his* livret de famille. *The young woman has refused to give the child away, and street disturbances against changing mores erupted in Ben M'sik, which were quickly quelled by the police. She was forced to flee with her child. Her whereabouts are unknown.*

The journalist didn't provide any further details about the woman's identity. But he did note that the young woman lived in Ben M'sik with her father, mother, and younger sister, and that she came from decent, hard-working stock. Her father was a factory worker who had become a mechanic, and her mother a secretary at a local high school.

*An unwed mother and her child, lacking legal rights and criminalized by the judicial system, are rejected and condemned by many. Their future is bound to be grim.*

But the writer didn't stop there. He concluded the article—and this was peculiar—with the child's name.

*The mother named the boy Noor.*

*Let us hope that light will soon follow the darkness.*

Nadine paused at that name: *Noor*, a name most often given to girls, one that means light, dawn, that moment when day breaks. How strange that this woman would call her son by a girl's name, and that the journalist would disclose the child's name. Was he unaware of the danger? Did he not know that once a name is made public, it can never be taken back?

It also seemed strange that a journalist—a male one at that—would bother to state that the father didn't register the child in his *livret de famille*. The very mention of this commonplace fact could be understood as a veiled criticism of the mother's and child's lack of rights, and that too was unusual. How often did a man ever legally recognize an illegitimate child?

She took out her phone and photographed the article, along with the journalist's name: Jamal Bidoun.

What an odd name, she thought. Jamal means beauty, and Bidoun without. Beauty Without—the one without beauty.

Perhaps he did know what was in a name.

Nadine wondered about the little boy, his whereabouts.

She imagined the softness of his almond eyes, the golden hue, perhaps, of his skin. She thought of another little boy and almost smelled him. She imagined a child who was like no other and like every other. She thought of the mother, the threaded words she would weave around her child like a gossamer blanket, her love, her fear, her probable despair. And, finally, she imagined the mother's strength and how great it had to be.

She felt she knew them, that somehow they were an intimate part of her. She also felt that in just an instant, her own life, like the lives of many women in her city and country, could tip over, and that she, out of blind chance, could be this woman, and this child could be her child; that her upper-class status, her resemblance to a European aristocrat, were a sham, an illusion. And that in one moment, she could be taken down from her pedestal and find herself just a woman among women, a being of lesser value, with lesser rights, in a country that still didn't know how to deal with, or think about, women.

She didn't think of the man. His need, his want, beyond consequence, protected by laws, ritualistic, held no interest or mystery to her.

Then Nadine heard a scratch and a scurry coming from the wall behind her. It had become a familiar sound—the sound of a lizard that lived in her walls. It stood still; its small head and tail half-raised, ready to run or hide. That, too, had become a familiar pose. Standing still, ready to run, too weak to attack yet trembling and determined, in a territory claimed as one's own, yet controlled by others.

She was tempted to kill it. It would be easy to do. Crushed by a book, by a loose mosaic tile, by the palm of her hand even, it was so thin and delicate. It was easy to kill weak creatures, to lose restraint, and let desire and want roll over you and wash everything clean.

# 3

# A Love Story

A lifetime ago, when Nadine and Kamal fell in love, they believed, like all couples, that their love was unparalleled, unique, eternal. They fell in love with one another easily and effortlessly. It was natural and good. Being in love is a state of grace that can't imagine its own absence.

While at first Nadine and Kamal believed that the stars had aligned to magically place them together, at the same party, on a specific night, at a particular time in their lives, they quickly came to believe the exact opposite: everything conspired to drive them apart. Everything and everyone were against them.

＊━━❦＊❦━━＊

When Kamal walked into his friend's apartment and saw Nadine in the middle of the crowd, he was drawn to her natural elegance. Sitting on the couch surrounded by her friends, her long, blonde hair was draped around one shoulder, her legs were crossed, and she held her cigarette like they do in the movies. He asked the party host who she was.

"Nadine Alam. Pretty much an orphan, dead mother, absent father, unapproachable. She says no to everyone.

Twenty-five years old, graduated from high school at sixteen. A newly minted doctor. A pediatrician. Too smart for you."

Kamal didn't need to hear anymore. He knew she was the one.

"Introduce us?"

"Brace for some broken bones."

Kamal laughed.

"We'll see."

He was fired up.

"Kamal Mesari is staring at you and he's coming our way," one of the young women sitting next to Nadine said to her with a mixture of envy and excitement.

"Who's Kamal Mesari?"

"Where have you been? Don't you ever go out?" the young woman stared at her. "Kamal Mesari is only *the* most available bachelor in town. Thirty-five years old, an architect, obviously handsome, and scion to the wealthy and powerful Ahensals on his mother's side."

Nadine frowned, intrigued.

"What's the catch?"

"He's a man," the young woman laughed, spilling her glass of red wine on the white couch. "That's the catch." She lowered her voice. "The mother. Word is that she's a dragon and blows real fire. Now hush, or he'll hear us."

———⌘———

When Kamal smiled at her, Nadine was ready to give him her heart, even though she was intelligent enough, knowledge-able enough, not to show him how she felt. Men liked the hunt, she had been told her entire life. And she meant to be respected and taken seriously.

But there was something deeper between them than a

simple hunting game or the right credentials. Nadine sensed his vulnerability and his deep-seated desire to do good, to be good. It was as though he had never been taught how and only a path forward was lacking.

As for Kamal, Nadine had a quality he had never encountered before and for which he could not find a better word than: unyielding. Beneath her golden beauty, there was a strength and an honesty that were practically nonexistent in his own social environment. Simply put, it was clear from the start that she was decent and cared deeply about being true to herself and to others. They clicked.

Their friends and social circles were approving enough that they didn't constitute an insurmountable hurdle, and critical enough that their story became deep and complex.

And so, their love grew like wildfire.

Their eyes mirrored the high esteem in which they held each other, and their image, reflected in their beloved, made them kinder, better, more accomplished individuals. It was irresistible, their assurance that their love would raise them higher, that it would nourish their better selves. That the afflictions of history—of their families, their city, their country—would never blind them to this goodness that carried such promise.

It was a love story worth living.

# 4
# Worlds within the Walls

Yet, the house Nadine lived in with Kamal had become a cold house. For those who inhabited it, there was a sense that the house would never become familiar, that they would never find peace, or safety, inside its walls. The house wasn't made to be a home.

There was another house, one old and beloved, small and strong, on Butterfly Street, on the other side of town, which no one knew she owned. She had hidden its existence from all of them—from him, her husband, first and most of all.

---

The house on Butterfly Street was Nadine's legacy, inherited from her mother, Alia Raiss, who herself inherited it from her mother, Maryam Peña. The manner by which Maryam Peña had acquired such a house was the stuff of legend, spanning histories and defying tradition.

Maryam, seeing that her husband was about to abandon her and her little daughter, had asked for it from her father, the Jewish Moroccan patriarch Abraham Peña. He had gone to live in New York City after shunning his daughter for marrying a Moroccan Muslim he deemed unfit for her in all ways. And that was Nadine's other well-kept secret: she was Jewish under Jewish law, and Muslim under Muslim law. And so Nadine lived in her husband's house, with that other house tucked inside her, hidden from view.

In this soulless house that belonged to her husband, the lights were too bright, corners had become angular embodiments of themselves, and the loft-like living-room was furnished to impress others, not to live in. This was a house that had turned its back on the past, on its doubts and shadows, its saints, devils and relics, completely and triumphantly. This was a house where there was nowhere to hide, to ponder deeply, nowhere to rest. Except for one mirror.

In Nadine's room, above the cherry wood dressing table on which she placed her hairbrush, makeup, and dark-blue and pink crystal jewelry box, hung a mirror. It was an antique that she claimed she had bought at the antiquaries in the Mozart Passage. But in truth, it had belonged to her mother, and to her grandmother before that, and she had sneaked it into her current bedroom from the well-kept secret that was her house on Butterfly Street.

⁕───❈───⁕

Nadine closed her eyes against the brutal morning light and called out to Amber, whom she could hear working in the kitchen, near the staircase leading to the family rooms that were situated on the second floor. She called to her by that forbidden name, *Dada,* that evil name according to historians, but one with which she had grown up, and in which she had placed her trust and her child's love—an intransigent, selfish love, as children's loves can be. A love that lay curled in the word she used for her, that existed in that hazy space between a mother and a father, that bridged and soothed a child's fears and a tender-less childhood. What connection could her love for the old Dada have with an archaic, adult institution that held other human beings in lifelong bondage?

And hadn't Dada's life been a good one? Hadn't she been loved and cared for, her entire life, never worrying about food in her belly or a roof over her head? And if Dada's life was a bondage, wouldn't Nadine's be one too, trapped as she was in the cold house with the cold husband, and nowhere to go?

She opened her eyes.

"Dada, come," she called to her again. "Where is Ghalia? Is she still not back?"

<hr />

Amber walked in, her feet slow, her bright, gray eyes searching the room from behind thick glasses. She sat down next to Nadine, her back cracking as she did so, her shoulders low, and she took the other woman's smooth hand in her own gnarled and crooked one.

"Something wicked came her way," Amber said. "Her family is silent. I fear she is burning her way out of the country."

"Burning?" Nadine repeated. "Ghalia is a bright young woman, studying for her engineering exam. She only worked here to pay her keep at her family's. Why would she risk her life in an illegal crossing?"

Amber kept quiet, nodding her head. A maid who was an engineering student, possessing a pride and beauty that a scullery maid shouldn't, was dangerous for all.

"She's a strange bird," Amber cautioned. "She could do or be anywhere. She has a mind of her own, plans. Maybe she's not who we thought she was. Maybe she deceived us."

Nadine shook her head.

"No, Ghalia's not like that. It's something else."

"We think we know others, but they remain a mystery to us."

Amber let go of Nadine's hand as a dark shadow flickered in her mind's eye, for she could see things others could not, and darkness filled her heart.

She didn't know the outside world, and she feared it. Amber had never been in the outside world, really. She hadn't known anything except the households of three generations of Peña women. And her outings were few and far between: no more than what can be counted on one hand. And no one ever knew where she had been on those days.

"Danger is close, I fear. Beware, little one, what you seek. Things are not as they seem."

The sun's glare was bright, the marble table under Nadine's fingers cold.

As a young woman, Nadine had read the story of a Chinese emperor who would pull the gold chain of a gold and emerald bell. Immediately the floor would open, and a sumptuous, elaborate meal would rise from the hollows of the kitchens below ground. But then the view shifted to the cooks and kitchen aides below who worked day and night. Some died of exhaustion or were punished for the slightest delay in opening the floor. And so the dark and complicated bondage of those below ground, who were expected to produce magic at the flick of a hand, was revealed.

"What are you hiding, Dada?"

"My knowledge has always been a twisted beast. It won't serve you."

Amber knew of the monsters that haunted houses. She had seen them as a child in her first Master's house, then as a young woman with only her mother to shield her from evil, her mother whose shielding arms had not been enough, for they were forced out of that first house—they were her cursed birthright. And so she knew what monsters haunted this one. She knew houses such as theirs were done and undone by a woman's hold over its Master.

Amber never mentioned Nadine's husband by name. It was always "he" or "Sidi," ("Sir") or "Master," but Nadine knew who she was referring to. She could sense it in the hatred and suspicion in Amber's voice, an ancient suspicion and hatred bred in wars and raids and rapes, in imposed obedience and docility, lurking beneath every mended shirt and washed sheet.

"There is a plague on my house. I sense it," said Nadine.

Her voice became soft and gentle, as it rarely was anymore.

"And my daughter, though she won't speak, senses it."

She glanced at the staircase leading to her daughter's room.

"Believe what you must, but you are in danger," said Amber. "The danger always comes from the same place—the husband and the woman he wants."

Nadine shivered at these words.

"Is there something you wish to tell me? Are you hiding something from me?"

Amber retreated in her chair, fear and distrust in her eyes. Though she cared about Nadine, she wasn't to be duped. After all, it was women from Nadine's class who had committed the greatest betrayals, who had become their natural enemies, fighting each other for the same prize: the master and his house. Fighting to remain inside the house, shielded by its pillars and its rules, its pecking orders and its rituals, strategizing with womb and mind, body and amulets, poisons in foods and liquid acids in drinks, prayers to God and ancient spirits alike. Fighting for the only end that mattered: *staying within the walls of the house and under its protection.*

She answered simply.

"If you don't want to do it my way, fine. But find a way, little one. Protect yourself. Don't dig too deep."

"What have you heard, Dada?"

Amber swayed slightly.

"So little, almost nothing. But if there is a secret that's being kept, it's a cruel one, not yours to unlock."

Nadine was familiar with Amber's cryptic speeches, her belief in the occult, and her distrust of men. It was her prism, made of brutal color and shade, filled with horror and cunning. Nadine loved Amber. But she realized, for the first time, that she had never questioned whether Amber loved her back. And this sudden awareness of the unknowability of the other woman's love made Nadine suspect that everything, all her feelings and emotions, might just be illusions, distorted reflections of a female hierarchy whose importance she had chosen to ignore.

She leaned forward in her chair and rested her hand on the older woman's arm, as though seeking warmth and reassurance.

Nadine had lost her mother when she was a little girl, and her father had been quick to remarry. Amber was the closest thing to a mother she had ever known, and she thought her to be blindly loyal. But now, as she looked at the older woman sitting in front of her, her intelligent eyes, sorrowful hands, and cryptic words, Nadine doubted her understanding of their relationship. She doubted its innocence, its warmth, and doubted her own role in it. Had she too taken advantage of this woman she persisted in calling *Dada* even though she knew the word's brutal roots? Pressed by her own entrapments, she'd been unable to translate them into compassion.

She brought her chair closer to the other woman's chair and held Amber's hands in hers.

———❦———

Jeanne Ba abruptly came down the rectangular wooden stairs in the corner of the rectangular loft-like space and crossed the floor to where the two women were sitting, their backs to the large bay windows.

Jeanne was young, in her early twenties, according to the passport that Nadine and Kamal kept locked in their safe, lest it be stolen from her, or lest she run away. But she was strong and calm for her age, and had kept silent as her passport was, once again, taken from her. She needed to say something to Nadine.

Jeanne shivered, waiting to speak. In the nearly three years she'd been in this house, she was still affected by how cold and crooked it was. The walls were white and bare, but they curved inwards and cast a disturbing shadow on the floor. Did no one sense how twisted and strange it was? It was like being in a monster's rough, white belly.

"Madam," Jeanne said softly. "It's about Al."

"Hello, Zahra. Is Al awake?"

That foreign, alien name. Jeanne nodded.

"She's awake, but she had a difficult night."

"Why didn't you call me?"

"There was no need to bother you, Madam. It's always the same difficulties. I stay next to her, and it passes."

Something in Jeanne's voice made Nadine suspicious.

"But this time, there's something different?"

"Yes, but…"

"Go on."

"It probably means nothing. I shouldn't even tell you, come to you with so little…"

"Even if it's nothing, tell me."

Jeanne felt pity for Nadine, this mother who couldn't be a mother to her own child and who had been violently rejected by her daughter. For Al refused her touch, her words, her food, her very presence. But children don't reject their parents without reason, for isn't that the worst thing under the stars a child can do. Nadine must have sins of her own. You reap what you sow.

The daughter's illness had changed Jeanne's duties, from helper to nanny of a young woman almost her own age. Jeanne sensed the family's relief at the change. But she also felt the mother's instinctive hatred and jealousy when Al didn't reject her as she had all the others, as she had her own mother and father.

Jeanne knew all about mothers who couldn't protect their children, and of the sunken fractures caused by fear and helplessness. Her own mother, though her love was fierce and deep, was never able to protect her from the poverty she was born into. And here was a mother who perhaps hadn't tried hard enough. But it's a sin to judge others. Jeanne missed her own mother terribly. She knew the remedying power of prayer, and she prayed every night for her mother and for those little brothers and sisters she had left behind.

Jeanne knew why Al didn't push her away, as she did Nadine, but she kept it to herself. Al didn't reject her because Jeanne knew Al's nightmares to be true. She knew nightmares do come in the night to rob you of your soul, discard your body, and eat your heart. She knew nightmares were real and ends of time existed.

As Nadine waited for Jeanne's answer, she realized how

her life and her child's life were in hands such as hers. Women like Jeanne made their world possible.

"Is it the nightmares? Are they back?"

"She called for you."

"What do you mean?"

"Your daughter, she called for you."

"What did she say?"

"Mom."

"Are you certain?"

"I'm certain. She repeated it, many times."

"Al hasn't spoken a word for so long. Maybe this is just a nervous tic, a reflex."

Jeanne shook her head.

"No, it's something more. I can't tell you what it means, but it was on purpose. She grabbed my arm. She's asking for you."

Immediately, Nadine stood and crossed the room and went up the stairs, and Jeanne followed her. They walked across the long hallway to Al's room. At her daughter's closed door, Nadine paused.

What if Jeanne had been mistaken? What if Al's calling her was some leftover word from long ago, meaningless?

"I'm going in. Alone."

Jeanne nodded and Nadine opened the door.

---

Al stood next to her bed, thin, her face ashen.

She was seventeen years old. There was no valid physical explanation for her long silence. But it started the day she looked down at her underwear and found blood there.

Nadine walked into her daughter's room and crossed over to her. She hesitated, for Al had refused her touch repeatedly.

Then she embraced her and held her tightly in her arms.

Al didn't return her embrace, but neither did she push her away.

Nadine held her daughter long and hard, wondering how they could have lived without each other's touch for so long. After a while, Al pushed her gently away and sat on her bed. Nadine took the rocking chair that stood forgotten by the window and dragged it in front of her daughter. She sat down and looked at her.

Al sighed.

"Hi, Mom."

She spoke these two words with difficulty.

Nadine reached out and stroked her daughter's hair. Might a misspoken word alarm Al to retreat back into silence?

"Hello, beloved."

She waited.

"I'm here. Talk to me."

Al hesitated and shook her head. Instead, she took out one of her sketchbooks and pencils. The room was quiet except for the sound of pencil on paper. Then she turned the sketchbook toward her mother.

She had drawn two shadowy figures in a jagged corner, a small tombstone with flowers blooming around it, a tiny body on top, eyes closed, but lips half-open, and cheeks blown, a sleeping child on top of a tombstone, and a figure with her palm resting on the knob of a half-open door with thin straight lines coming through that seemed to Nadine to be filtered light shining through.

Then Al turned the page and wrote.

"Find Ghalia."

Nadine's heart beat faster. Her daughter's words mirrored her own questions.

"Why do I need to find Ghalia, Al?"

Al's expression was unreadable.

"To make things right."

Then she started sketching again, lost to the world.

Nadine kissed her softly on the forehead.

"My little girl. I'm so sorry. I'll make things right."

Al watched as her mother left the room.

---

"Please, Zahra," Nadine said to Jeanne who had been waiting outside Al's room. "Take care of her until I return. If the master asks for me, tell him I went to see my mother."

"But, your mother…"

"Is dead, I know. Just tell him."

Nadine walked back down the long hallway to her room. But Amber was standing in the way, fire in her eyes.

"I heard everything," Amber told her with anger in her voice. "You'll regret finding what you seek. Stay here, keep your eyes closed. Defend what's here."

"You hear what you choose to hear, Dada."

"I hear danger when it comes knocking, loud as an ogre in the middle of the night."

"I need to find Ghalia. She may be the key to everything that's wrong in this house. Why else would Al mention her? Why would she send me to find her?"

"A child, who thinks she sees and understands things that are beyond her young years and that have made her sick."

"I'll be back soon, with answers and, hopefully, with a cure to this poison that's inside my daughter."

Amber could feel, if not see, the walls of the house crumbling. She saw herself as she was: without a shell, forever alone. But not without tricks up her sleeve.

"Be careful. I hear the monsters out there are almost as vicious as the ones inside the walls," she warned.

Nadine walked into her room and closed the door.

---

Amber walked towards Al's room, to where Jeanne stood, her back against the wall, guarding the door. Amber tried to push past her, but found that she couldn't.

"Let me in. I need to know what Al thinks she saw, or knows."

"I can't. Her mother asked that she rests. And Al barely speaks again; and maybe she only spoke this one time because she needed to," said Jeanne.

"This isn't a home at all," Amber lashed out. "It's a hungry beast, at war with the women and children trapped in its belly. How many children must it break? I've been on this earth long enough."

"There are worse places than this," replied Jeanne softly. "I know of a place, a terrible, dangerous place. They trap people inside and smoke them out."

"What is this place?"

Jeanne lowered her voice even more.

"They call it *l'Enfumoir*. There are those who don't believe it's real, who think it's an old wives' tale. But I know it's real. And I fear that's where her search will take her."

Amber's eyes narrowed.

"And how do you, a foreigner, know of this place?"

Jeanne shook her head and retreated.

"I have heard people speak of it. That's all I know."

Amber stared at Jeanne before walking away, a world of distrust between them.

---

Alone in her room, Nadine sat in front of the cherry wood dressing table and mirror, her back to the door. She looked into the mirror, at her pale eyes and thin face, at the stranger she had become. She placed the newspaper clipping in front of her, smoothed out its wrinkles and again silently read the story to herself. She knew then that if she left the house, she would never be the same again. She touched the mirror and felt its cool, comforting hardness against her fingertips. I'll always be here, it seemed to promise. Time, like an accordion, stretched and compressed inside its reflection, beyond the scope of a lifetime.

She slid the newspaper into her purse, grabbed her keys, and walked out of her room, down the stairs, and out the front door.

Closing the door behind her, she didn't look back at all.

# Part II

# 5

# The Apartment

*Early that afternoon*

Nadine drove from her house in Casablanca's Palmiers district to the sprawling neighborhood of Ben M'sik on the city's fringes. With its population of one hundred sixty thousand souls, Ben M'sik was more a town unto itself than a neighborhood on the fringes of a large city. A sprawling, historic quadrangle surrounded by other sprawling working-class neighborhoods, it was its own world. Ben M'Sik, known for its Jewish cemetery, its Christian cemetery, its university, its massive Kariane bidonville (the city's largest shantytown, until its demolition in 2015), was a turbulent, crime-ridden, threatening part of the city that Nadine, and people like her, tried to avoid.

But Ben M'sik was home for Ghalia and her family. And Nadine needed to find out what happened to the young woman, her housekeeper for almost two years, a stranger, yet a girl whose fate had prompted Nadine's daughter, Al, to speak after almost two years of silence.

Nadine crossed from large, palm-tree filled avenues and well-manicured parks to narrow streets, hemmed in by looming buildings stuffed tightly together on either side. A jumble of humanity, the only persistent presences were the beggars at every traffic light and crossing: women carrying little children on their backs or holding them by the hand, West African refugees and migrants, Syrian refugees, handicapped children pushed in wheelchairs by a man or woman who barely glanced at them as they went from car to car.

It was at red lights and crossings, thought Nadine, as she fumbled to find a dirham or two to give to whomever came first to her window, or had a child, that the city's misery appeared. Red-headed Syrian refugees, who, even after the war in Syria had officially ended, were too scared or impoverished to return home. Malian, Ivorian, Nigerian, and Sudanese migrants and refugees, with small children on their backs or at their sides, small children as young as five out on their own, old men and women, the physically and mentally impaired, young men without any visible affliction except for a wild, hollow look in their eyes, Moroccan women with their children, sometimes newborns.

Some people in Nadine's circle of friends, manipulated by news coverage, questioned whether the children were mostly orphans used by a professional panhandling network to soften people's hearts into giving more. After all, what mother would use her own child to beg at red lights, sometimes at midnight, when it's cold and the streets are at their toughest? But Nadine looked at the way these women held the babies in their arms and thought: this is clearly a mother, holding her child in such a way, soft and strong, so that the child is warm against her. Though she did wonder if that child, lying limp in the woman's arms, were even alive and if the mother knew. Then anger filled her: where was the father, the ever-absent father?

Red light after red light of empty, outreached hands, stumbling words uttered in languages that were not theirs, and new street smarts written in the rubble of memories revealing how a life can slip from safety to peril in an instant. *It could be me,* Nadine thought. *I may be worlds apart from these people, but it could be me. Just like that, everything can crack.* She turned on the radio to numb herself to an encroaching fear as she drove.

⁕⁕⁕

Ben M'sik was a rectangular city spread. It wasn't as alien as the chasms created by words had led her to believe. With its crooked buildings and broken sidewalks, its fruit and vegetable carts, pedestrians and stray cats, but also new tram lines and large avenues, in some ways it was actually a typical Casablanca neighborhood. She could be anywhere in the city. And yet, its feel changed from street to street: safe to unsafe, familial to gang-controlled. There was this sense here that a spark could flare up in an instant, destroying everything in its passage. At the same time, there was also a bustling serenity, easy flows of people and conversations, a sense of belonging in these fringes that throbbed like village markets.

Nadine stopped at a bakery on the way to pick up a cake. As she got close to the address, she parked the car on the corner of Boulevard Ibn Khattab and looked for building number 114, the home address Ghalia had given when she first started working for her.

Casablanca's streets often had the names of ancient male Arab heroes, poets, and explorers. In the outlying neighborhoods, built either for the needs of the first French industries or to quickly house the many displaced Casablanca residents after the destruction of the slums by the city, it was either the

many names of heaven and joy or simply street numbers—
Rue 1, Rue 2. In the more central neighborhoods, often built
by the French, the streets still carried the names of flowers,
animals, colonial administrators, or obscure French men
and military officers. But not once had Nadine ever seen the
name of a woman on a Casablanca street.

⸻ ❦ ⸻

Building 114 was pink, stout, and five-storied, with its
number painted in white on the front. The front door was
ajar. Nadine, her arms carrying cake and Ghalia's belongings,
pushed it open with her shoulder and walked in.

Though the sun shone brightly outside, it was dark
inside, for the hallway lights had long-since flickered and
died, and no one had replaced them. There was no elevator, so
she turned on her phone light and started up the stairs to the
second floor. There was a dank smell to the place, but despite
that, it seemed clean enough. She didn't come across anyone,
as if the building were deserted. It's a work day, she thought
to herself. Parents are at work and kids at school. It wasn't yet
five o'clock. And she had lost track of work days and school
days. She controlled her apprehension and continued up the
steps to Apartment 4C.

There were five apartments on each floor. Apartment 4C
was on the second floor, on the far right corner and had a
knocker: a broken brass hand of Fatima. She hesitated, then
curled her fingers around the broken brass hand and knocked.

A very young girl opened the door.

She was thin and pale. From her torn plastic sandals,
knotted scarf around her head, and red, wet hands, Nadine
understood she must be the family's maid. She appeared to
be no older than twelve. The young maid's eyes widened at

the sight of the well-dressed woman at the door. She smiled at Nadine hesitantly, her eyes lighting up her face.

Just a child, thought Nadine. But she knew of these families who would hire little girls for a hundred dirhams a week, work them to the bone, and claim their ward as a charity they performed for very poor families in need of money. Families—both poor and wealthy—would groom little girls into becoming maids, akin to slaves. The money, if one could call it that, went straight to their families.

Nadine smiled at her.

"Are your people home?"

The little girl nodded and asked her to please wait at the door. She quickly returned with an older man. He was dark-skinned, very tall, and thin. His face was marked and wrinkled, and his eyes tired. Only his hands were beautiful and full of vigor. He was probably much younger than he looked.

"Who are you and what do you want?"

"Are you Allal Ait Iddin, Ghalia's father?"

"Who's asking? You're a journalist?"

*A journalist?* Nadine felt sick.

"No, I'm not…"

"We've had our share of journalists. We just want to be left alone."

"Mr. Ait Iddin, my name is Nadine Mesari. I'm your daughter Ghalia's employer. She hasn't come to work for almost a month, and she doesn't answer her phone. I was worried about her. I came to see if she's okay."

Allal Ait Iddin gave her a strange look. Nadine couldn't tell whether it was one of fear, hatred, or despair. Nevertheless, she understood she wasn't welcome here.

Then a woman came to the door. She was heavy-set, with cold eyes, and dressed in a blue cotton *djellaba*. She had smooth, white skin and aquiline features that suggested she must have been very beautiful once, before coldness beset her eyes and bitterness her mouth.

"Mrs. Mesari, Ghalia's fine. She's studying for her exams and won't be able to come work for you anymore. I'm sorry she didn't let you know. We thought she had."

There was something brutal in the way this woman spoke. A brutality that perhaps wasn't natural but was meant to hide something. Nadine tried again.

"May I come in? I mean no harm. I'm simply concerned," she added with a smile, "and I have a cake."

The woman hesitated, looked at the cake, then slowly nodded, opening the door for her.

———⟨⟩———

Nadine left her shoes in the front hallway and walked into the apartment. The floor was plastic linoleum that imitated mosaics, and the space was small and sparsely furnished. But it was clean and well kept, the little girl's doing.

She followed the couple into the living room, the main room of the house, with red-and-gold embroidered couches lining the walls, used by family members visiting from the countryside to sleep on when they came into the city. Low, carved wooden tables sat atop a bright Berber carpet. Lace curtains adorned the small windows, and a tea platter was set on one of the side tables.

The kitchen was to the right. The stove, fridge, sink, and faucet were old and used, but were wiped clean by the hand of the child. In one corner of the kitchen was a bare mattress. Where this child must sleep, thought Nadine, as she watched the young maid put the cake on a plate and bring forks and knives to the table.

To the right was a smaller room with a TV, and to the left was a hallway leading to three bedrooms and a bathroom.

The walls were painted a light shiny pink, and they were bare except for three things: a large black cloth with a verse from the Quran in gold embroidery, a portrait of the king, Mohamed VI, as a young man, and a portrait of a young bride and groom. The bride, beneath her heavy makeup, looked young, barely eighteen. She gazed straight ahead into the camera, and thin, shiny cracks could be seen through the makeup. The groom was an old man.

There was a time, before the little boy died inside her, when Nadine was a young medical student and new doctor. Her rounds would take her across the city, and she would see families and homes that were worlds apart from her own. So she had seen enough to know that the Ait Iddin household wasn't a poor one. It belonged to that ill-defined and ever-changing category called the urban middle classes.

But that was a lifetime ago, when her presence among strangers was seen as a blessing, for doctors were magical beings, believed to cure all ills and wrongdoings.

Parents presented their children to her, their cheeks red and their foreheads damp. Old men and women came to ease the pain of still being alive. Women, eyes lowered and hands damp, came to have her look at bruises and cuts on their arms, stomachs and thighs, well-hidden from the eyes of the world. Men came with nervous tics and rashes that they thought were caused by a jealous wife, a jilted lover, an enemy who was owed money, whose anxiety hindered all sleep and all work. Nadine felt the usefulness, and the futility, of her work, then. Human suffering was endless, but she sometimes could put a balm on wounds, while she oscillated between pride in a task well done and despair at the depth of the anguish that escaped the bounds of the medical field.

But on this day, not needed, not wanted, she was trespassing. She was a stranger to this world, which she no longer needed to think of until one month ago, when Ghalia, the honest, hard-working young woman who worked for her as a maid, disappeared.

———— ✽ ————

Nadine sat down and a tray of sweets was set before her. Lamis Ait Iddin cut the cake, while Allal poured the tea into thin blue glasses.

Nadine began carefully.

"Ghalia mentioned her exams were coming up and that, if she passed them, she wouldn't work at our house anymore. But I thought the exams weren't for another three months, at least. In June, is that correct?"

"She's behind in her work. Distracted lately. We told her it's best to concentrate on her studies," came Lamis Ait Iddin's curt reply.

"But, forgive my asking, she needed the money, did she not?"

When the mother looked at Nadine again, she couldn't quite read her expression, as she couldn't with the father's before her. Her eyes held something between anger and fear, but also surprise, and curiosity.

"Ma'am. Life isn't always easy for the likes of us, but we do our best. We have pride, you know."

"Of course. I meant no disrespect. It just doesn't make sense. And Ghalia is a sensible girl. May I see her?"

"She's not here. We sent her to the countryside to concentrate on her exams. It's best."

The long silence was interrupted only by the sounds of tea being sipped and the knife hitting the plate as it cut through the cake.

Nadine then asked her next question as carefully as she could.

"Mr. Ait Iddin, you asked me earlier, when I was at the door, if I were a journalist. Why?"

Avoiding his wife's angry stare, Allal Ait Iddin came up with an answer.

"I don't recall…If I did, it's because journalists often come to Ben M'sik to ask about the destruction of the Karian, or our reactions to the latest crime. As though all of Ben M'sik were filled with criminals, or the displaced from the Karian. This neighborhood is as quiet and honorable as yours, Mrs. Mesari." There was despair in his voice, a plea even.

"I'm sure of it, Mr. Ait Iddin. But it seemed, from your words, that lately, they've been coming often. That, in fact, they came to you directly."

"I must have given you the wrong idea. Why would a journalist have anything to do with a simple mechanic like me?" he said, showing her the palms of his strong, bruised hands.

Nadine sipped her tea and glanced at the portrait of the young bride and her middle aged groom. She noticed she had short hair, which was strange for a bride, and rare for a young girl. Her hair was unruly and the bride's tiara barely kept her curls in place.

"Is this young woman a relation?"

"That's our youngest daughter…Yasmina," he answered, pausing slightly.

"Do you have many children?"

"Two daughters, Yasmina and Ghalia. Yasmina just got married."

There was unease in the father's voice. Nadine thought she even heard sadness.

"Yasmina married a family friend. An old friend of mine, and some relation to my wife. He went to Belgium and made a fortune there. She's living with his parents now, but he'll soon come get her and she'll live in Belgium."

The mother nodded.

"Yasmina's husband is a relation of ours," she added. "His family is kin to mine, so we know she's in good hands. It's still best for girls to get married to a good man. School and studying, it takes too long and not everyone can make it."

"But with school, a woman has more security, more independence, and that's a good thing, too, isn't it?" Nadine asked.

She realized that the couple were in fact around the same age as Kamal and herself, not older, as she had first thought. They stared at her, and again, that anger, that helplessness in their eyes.

"Do you have children, Ma'am?" the mother asked.

"I have one daughter."

"No son, like us?"

"No, no other child."

Lamis leaned toward her, her eyes filled with a strange hunger and greediness.

"No sons then? Ah a woman without a son. Isn't that the worst? A half-mother, always, a half-woman, always. Isn't it so? Even for the likes of you? A son, the ultimate gift!"

The hatred and fire in her now were undeniable.

"Your beautiful house, your charmed life, your rich husband who does as he pleases, to whomever he pleases. But no son, huh? Anyone can grab it from you, take it all just like that."

She snapped her fingers, sat back, an infinite sorrow echoing around her.

"Just like me. In the end, you're just like me," she went on. "A mother to daughters, a mother to weakness. And no woman, at all, for you don't know what's coming, do you?"

And she started laughing—a long, shrill, uncontrollable laughter.

Lamis Ait Iddin, the cold, inscrutable assistant to a sprawling private high school that bled local parents dry with extravagant fees and lowly quality, once beautiful, now tired and bitter, never showed her feelings to strangers, nor did she ever reveal what it was that haunted her and kept her awake at night. But in front of this neatly dressed woman, her blonde hair in a ponytail, her sophisticated perfume and kind eyes, she lost it. And the chaos she had battled every day and every night, the frustration born of humiliation, of being overlooked and denied, despite all her physical gifts, finally took over, its noose firmly attached around her neck.

The couple, their guest, and the little girl who served them just sat there, lost in their thoughts, unable to make sense of the outburst, unable to reach out to each other, or to provide comfort to each other.

Nadine finally interrupted the silence.

"I would never hurt your daughter. I would never hurt anyone, not knowingly."

Allal Ait Iddin got up, signaling the visit was over.

Nadine stood up as well. But before leaving, she made one final attempt.

"Here's my number," she said to them both. "If Ghalia needs anything, or if she wishes to return, tell her to contact me. Please let me know if I can help in any way."

The mother's expression remained inscrutable, cold and closed, but the father looked at her with hope, slight, but there it was, in the shadow of his eyes. He opened his mouth, but immediately closed it again.

Nadine gave the mother the bundle of clothes, soap, and comb that Ghalia had left at the house. Lamis and Allal Ait Iddin watched, in silence, as she walked out the door and down the stairs.

⸻ ⬩⬦⬩ ⸻

Nadine knew they had lied to her. And she wondered why, since she was there to help. Unless it was because they didn't trust her. Because there was some kind of danger. Because it had some connection to her.

As she was about to reach her car, someone tugged at her arm. Turning around, she saw the Ait Iddin's little maid. Younger than her own daughter, there was that admiration in her eyes she saw earlier.

"You really don't know, Ma'am?"

"What should I know, little one?"

The little girl hesitated, then spoke.

"I think you're nice. You smell nice, and your eyes are gentle. Even when you're angry. Maybe you can help her. She was nice too, and she talked about you a lot. She would give me sweets and hot milk and a comforter when the nights were cold."

She slipped a piece of paper into Nadine's hands.

"I can't read, but the gentleman who gave me this said that if I hear anything, to go to the corner store and they'd call this number for me. But I'm too scared."

"What are you scared of?"

"I have to go. They don't like it when I stay out of the house too long."

"Okay. But tell me your name. I want to know who to say thank you to."

And the little girl's face lit up.

"My name is Itto. But they call me Zinab. The Ait Iddins don't want Berber names in the city, they say it's backwards. The Ait Iddins, they're not all bad. They're from my village. They just left a long time ago. They know my parents."

And she ran off, back through the black door and the dark, dank smelling hallway and up the unlit stairs and back into the apartment that she kept clean, and on whose linoleum kitchen floor she slept, her body on a bare mattress; back to the couple who kept her prisoner there, as are kept many little girls throughout the neighborhood, the city, the country. Back to what is called poverty.

Nadine looked at the piece of paper that Itto had slipped in her hands. Scribbled on it were a phone number and a name: Jamal Bidoun.

She hesitated. She could return to her quiet house in Palmiers and live the rest of her life as she had done. Or she could call this number with the knowledge that her life might never again be the same.

# 6
# The Office

Nadine stared at the piece of paper in her hands. A piece of paper with a number and a name that she had been the first to read, for Itto had never learned to read or write. It seemed to have landed in her hands because it had been meant for her from the start. Jamal Bidoun wasn't a name she could forget. It was the name of the journalist who had written about the young single woman from Ben M'sik who had refused to give up her newborn child for adoption and who then had been forced out of her home into the streets.

There was nothing unique in this news item. Casablanca is a city rife with stories of young single women who have had children out of wedlock. What caught Nadine's attention was the fact that the journalist had chosen to divulge the child's name, to acknowledge it. That could mean one of two things: he had met the mother or he had met someone who knew the child's name. In either case, by revealing that the child was named Noor—*light*, the light of early day— one could speculate that the child was loved enough to be given a name and that the mother, wherever she may be, would hold on to her child with all her strength.

Was there a link between Ghalia and the woman in the article? How could there be? Nadine would have noticed if Ghalia had been pregnant. And if she didn't, wouldn't Dada Amber or Zahra have noticed? But she recalled Dada Amber's last words to her before she left the house that morning: "Others remain a mystery to us. Things aren't as they seem."

Something else came to mind: the disdain and impatience with which Kamal had spoken to Ghalia over the last months before her disappearance. Kamal never hid his disgust with women who had relations with men outside of marriage. To hear him tell it, Casablanca is a city of loose women who trap men to secure their future. If they were stopped from using such tactics, the number of illegitimate children would dwindle. End of story.

Anyway, how could he have known about Ghalia?

Nadine sat in her car as the city's bustle crowded her thoughts. Across the horizon, a shaft of light filtered through the rainless gray clouds gathering over the ocean, casting buildings in unexpected brightness.

She took out her cell phone and dialed the number written on the piece of paper. Shortly, a male voice, quiet and cordial, answered.

"Jamal Bidoun here."

"Mr. Bidoun?"

"Yes."

"Mr. Bidoun, my name is Nadine Mesari. I was given your number by Itto, the little girl employed by the Ait Iddins. She said you gave her your number..."

"Hello, Mrs. Mesari. Ah yes, Itto. A sweet child."

"She said you could help me."

"Or maybe you can help me."

Nadine hesitated, then continued.

"I'm looking for a young woman who used to work for me. The Ait Iddins' daughter, Ghalia Ait Iddin. She hasn't been back to work for a month, and it's not like her. Her parents claim she's in the countryside with some relatives studying for her exams. I have trouble believing them."

There was a pause on the other side of the line. Then the man's voice lost some of its easy tone, becoming more formal and distant.

"I remember your name, now—Mesari. What is it you want with this young woman, Mrs. Mesari?"

"I want to see if she's okay."

"Why would someone like you bother with her?"

"I'm concerned about her. This isn't like her to disappear."

"...Listen, I think I believe you. Come to the office."

He gave her the address.

"I'll wait for you," he said, before hanging up without a goodbye.

He wasn't a man of many words, thought Nadine. But there was something reassuring behind his brusque, quiet way of speaking.

Dusk was falling on the city in pinks, purples, and delicate yellows, colors diffused by the low-hanging clouds, the glistening ocean, and the thick smoke of the factories.

The address he gave her was a side street connecting to the Park of the Arab League, the city's largest and most beloved park: *42 Rabi'a Al Adawiya Street, 3rd floor.*

It was a street named after a woman, the first Casablanca street named after a woman she had ever seen.

Nadine knew little about her and was surprised that the administration and the men behind the naming of streets and mounting of street signs had considered her to be great enough, or nonthreatening enough, or transcendent enough, to allow her to reign supreme on a side street to one of the most central city squares.

At this time of day, it would take her an hour to get there. She turned on the ignition and drove off.

———❦———

The city spread out around and ahead of her, its rundown buildings and decrepit art-deco and Hispanic-Moorish style buildings giving way to 1970s monstrosities and thin green parks that snaked through the city's center.

By the time she arrived at the Park of the Arab League, the sun had almost set, and the streets were almost deserted. The Park of the Arab League, built in colonial times, had recently been renovated. Now, for the first time in thirty years, it closed itself to the night and to the city's wandering, high-on-drugs and cold-with-suffering, aimless men, women, and children. Instead, it provided a greener, more manicured, more policed, and well-tended space for families and students to congregate in.

Nadine hadn't been in this neighborhood for a very long time. How beautiful it was during those briefest of moments when city dwellers turned on the lights in their homes and the streets breathed a little, empty and quiet; the moments just before night took over, rendering the city center even more distinctive, with its decorative architecture and iconic markets. But it also became even more threatening and solitary, abandoned by almost everyone except its most desperate, or bravest.

Nadine turned right onto the narrow side street Rabi'a Al Adawiya, leaving the park behind her. In front of address number forty-two, a shapeless office building, derelict and in poor state, she stopped and parked.

She got out of the car and turned to look at the park. On its outer edge was the city's cathedral, built by colonial architects in a stocky style that was countered by a delicate whiteness and elegant stained glass. And there, in the center of the park was the refined building of white marble and green tiles, erected in honor of the city's Islamic scholars, where her father would take her on Sunday mornings. Before her mother died and he became too busy.

———✴———

She entered the building that housed the newspaper office for which Jamal Bidoun worked.

Getting into the elevator, Nadine pressed the button for the third floor. At the door to the newspaper's office sat an elderly man, a security guard. Half asleep, he stood up as she approached and opened the door behind him. He seemed to have been expecting her.

*Les Nuits Casablancaises* was a well-known newspaper, with a decent enough distribution still. So Nadine was surprised to see that the office consisted of an eight-person conference room, four small-sized rooms, and a shared workspace that could hold ten people at most. The office was empty. Cardboard boxes lined the floor, computers were packed in boxes on the tables, and the lights were off, except for a cold overhead light buzzing in the hallway and the light coming from behind a closed door at the end of the hallway. It seemed no one worked here.

The security guard pointed to the door at the end of the hallway and returned to his seat by the door. Nadine walked cautiously up to the door, and knocked. The voice of the man she'd spoken with on the phone told her to enter.

———✴———

Jamal Bidoun was seated at his desk in a cloud of cigarette smoke, his square glasses peering into the computer's blue screen. Behind him, large windows overlooked the park, the fading bustle of cars below, and the street lights that had just lit up. When he saw her, he stood up, a hand extended, a smile warming his face.

Jamal Bidoun wasn't what Nadine expected. He looked like an ordinary working man, weathered by time, sun and labor, rather than a journalist or Casablanca intellectual.

He must have been in his seventies, his hair was completely gray. Jamal wasn't tall, but he was thick and heavyset. If it weren't for his warm smile and kind, twinkling eyes, he might seem somewhat terrifying, despite his age. But he exuded both strength and kindness, a scarce combination, and he held her hand in his for a long time, as though certain it would give him a glimpse into her very soul.

Despite his gruff appearance and mildly painful, bearlike handshake, Nadine sensed this man was decent and good, and a force of nature.

His contagious smile widened. Jamal pulled out a chair for her by the window and turned his chair toward her. Before sitting down, he offered her coffee.

"Coffee at this hour?" she asked.

"At any hour."

Nadine nodded, and as he prepared the coffee, she took in the surroundings. In the beleaguered newspaper business, suffering from dwindling funds and readership, in which most staff usually had to share open work spaces, Jamal Bidoun had his own office. How could a journalist whose single column was on the back page of the paper get such an office?

He handed her a cup of coffee and motioned to the mosaic of light and steel beyond the windows.

"Pretty nice, isn't it?"

"A corner office…you must have the best view of anyone here."

"All surface, this city. Appearances, image. Its beauty at night hides crumbling buildings and lives. Just like my office hides the end of script and newspapers."

"I don't understand."

He shrugged. "Newspapers are dying. We think people want to really know what's what. They don't."

"They want entertainment?"

"They want to *be* entertainment. They want their time in the spotlight. We've had ours, our great fight. And it's over."

"But here you are. And you wrote an article that brought me right to your doorstep," said Nadine, gently. It was hard not to respect this old reporter.

"Did you notice the name of the street we're on, Mrs. Mesari?"

"Rabi'a Al Adawiya. Sounds familiar. Who is she?"

"Rabi'a of Basra. Muslim saint and illuminated Sufi mystic."

"And here she is, on a street sign."

"And here she still is," Jamal repeated, quietly. "Eighth century, stolen as a child, sold as a slave. Only to rise to become one of the greatest thinkers and religious leaders of her time. A person of power."

"And the only woman, I think, whose name is on one of our city's street signs. But why are you telling me this?"

"*Differences exist, but not in the city of love. Thus my vows and yours, I know they are the same…*Her words."

Nadine shifted in her seat as the sun set, and they were left in the quiet twilight of the office.

"Mr. Bidoun, I came here because…"

"Call me Jamal and I will call you Nadine, if you will allow me. I know why you came."

"Okay…Jamal. Then you know I'm here to find out what happened to Ghalia Ait Iddin. I was told you could help me. If you don't wish to help me, then please just say so."

Jamal looked at Nadine, a quizzical look in his eyes. He pulled on his cigarette and offered her one.

"Since you're here, you must be brave. And kind. How brave and kind are you prepared to be?"

"I need to find out where she is. That's the most important thing for me to do at this moment. Perhaps the most important thing I will ever have to do," she said.

"Honest, too! Well then, Nadine Mesari, tell me this. Do you know why *bastard* is not a nice word?"

Nadine pulled back.

Jamal's smile illuminated his face. But Nadine thought she saw a raging anger in his black eyes, or was it a permanent sadness.

"You're a kind soul, Nadine. Do you know why it's a terrible word in this country? Because it unloads all the blame on the child, and the mother. The child bears the burden of the father's abandonment. Of the state's hypocrisy. And so does the mother. And neither will survive that word, or ever escape from it. There are other terrible words—maid, dada, 'abid, slave, slut, homo, illegal, migrant. But *bastard*, that's the father of all shit words, the coat of arms of violence."

Nadine was beginning to think Jamal Bidoun had no intention of giving her the information she needed, and was possibly insane. She would try one last time, then she would leave.

"Jamal, what do you know about Ghalia Ait Iddin?"

A smile, genuine and deep, crept slowly across his face:

"Good. You don't get sidetracked. What do you want to know?"

"Where is she?"

"How do I know you're not looking to hunt her down?"

"Would I be here—by myself—if I wanted to do that? And why would I want to hunt her down?…"

He looked out the window.

"I'm closing shop. This newspaper was mine. It's dead. It was our last week. Everybody has left except for the watchman at the door and myself, once a scourge on the state, now old and out of shape…and then you show up."

"You're the publisher! Why are you closing?"

"We've been hanging on by a thread. The company that bought it wants to move it all online and make it into a business paper. That's not what I do. I'm a newsman—an old-fashioned newsman. I write about the unfair treatment of people. I want my words to change bad things, not just report them. And I can't pay the fines anymore. I've done the jail time. I'm too old now. And that article was the final straw for them."

"For whom?"

"The police. I refused to tell them where the woman and her child had gone to. The fine was too high. The newspaper was pretty much over, and that killed it."

Jamal paused.

"As usual, there's someone powerful behind all this. Someone directly involved, who has the money to hunt down those who don't wish to be found, who could be a nuisance to him."

"You're saying someone's behind the police call. Do you know who that might be?"

Jamal shifted in his chair.

"What does it matter? I wrote that article as a goodbye to a life of fighting and informing and reporting. And I wrote down that child's name as a father would write down his child's name in the state registry. To legitimate him. Noor. And it has brought you here. And that's something."

"You say this child brought me to you, but you haven't answered any of my questions."

"I've been answering all your questions. Maybe even more than you want."

"I want to understand it all. And what does it have to do with me?"

"Do you really want to come with me and see this woman and her child? See what's happened to them?"

"Who is she?"

"You know who she is. You've known from the start. That's why you're here."

Nadine was certain he was mistaken. She hadn't known anything from the start, and she hadn't seen anything.

But then one person came to mind. A person who had disappeared, who was from Ben M'sik, who was brave and young.

"Ghalia." Nadine said.

"Would you like to go see her?"

---

Nadine followed Jamal out the door, across the empty office floor, and out the building. The security guard was nowhere to be seen.

Jamal stopped and turned to look at the building that had housed the newspaper for over thirty years, an indecipherable expression on his face.

"Even with all its flaws and sins, we still love our city, no?" he asked Nadine quietly.

She looked at him in surprise. It was a long time since she had thought of her city in those terms. But yes, behind and despite the anger and fear, there was love.

They walked away.

Then that great smile again as he pointed to a beat-up, nineties Peugeot 206.

"That used to be my car."

"Whose is it now?"

"I gave it to this kid who always helped me change my tires when they got slashed by you can guess who. My parting gift."

"How will you get around?"

"Cabs or tram, like any modern citizen. But not tonight. Tonight, we need a car."

They walked toward her car. As they buckled their seatbelts, Jamal turned to Nadine.

"Those words, *differences exist, but not in the city of love. Thus my vows and yours, I know they are the same.* I believe Rabi'a Al Adawiya wrote them for people like you or me. For someone like you, with a solitude like yours, and someone like me, with a solitude like mine. To meet and work together."

# 7

## The Center

Nadine's face was firmly set. The lines around her mouth and eyes were visible and deep under the moonlit sky and bland streetlights. Until Jamal had climbed into the car and given her directions, she still had hope. Despite the darkness and anger settling in her bones, she had prayed that she wouldn't need to go down this road. She should have stayed in the relative comfort of her life, looking at the world from afar, in the safety of her own home, in the unawareness that was the basis of her security and her marriage. She should have kept things as they were. After all, pecking orders have existed since the beginnings of time, and for a reason. They worked.

They drove toward the *Quartier des Hôpitaux*, home to the city's public hospital buildings. Getting closer to the women's center, they drove through the surrounding, impoverished neighborhood of small, aging houses, bustling streets lined with orange and lemon trees, fifty-year-old gas stations, and brand-new, family-sized supermarkets with Turkish or French names.

Most of the houses were old and decrepit. Speculators had started buying them up. In some of the larger streets, developers had already cut down the fruit trees, demolished the neglected, narrow cobblestone sidewalks, and started tearing down the small houses, replacing them with cheap-looking, five-story apartment buildings, falsely advertised as *"luxury"* and *"super luxury."* Their extravagant prices were displayed on huge billboards, and under their shadow stood the homeless, asking passersby for a dirham or two.

Nadine's pale green eyes became even paler in the light of the moon. She realized that this neighborhood mirrored her own. It wasn't far from it, but it was a world apart: a failing gentrification, of older, poorer, inhabitants. Both landscapes were equally heartbreaking.

And yet, some of the neglected streets had an ineffable vibe that Palmiers had lost to forward-thinking architects and ambitious promoters. Neighbors still congregated on sidewalks, street vendors were plentiful, and children played outside. It still had soul.

Following Jamal's directions, Nadine turned into a side street that rounded into a dead end, called Rue H. They had reached their destination.

"Park wherever you can," he said. "Your car is too big for the city," he added, chuckling.

Nadine found a parking space she could slide her car into. She opened her car door to get out.

"Nayla Dani may not be like other women you're used to," Jamal said to her. "But you can trust her. I always have."

<hr />

The center was a squat, square house nested in the middle of the dead end, its light blue façade wet and curling from humidity and lack of maintenance. To the side of its rusty, black, wrought-iron gate was a sign: *Maryam Al-Fihriya Center for Women and Children.*

Nadine walked around the car and stood next to Jamal. He stared at her, as if making sure she hadn't changed her mind. Satisfied by what he saw, a warm, encouraging smile lit his face.

The night-guardian, an old man in traditional clothes and Adidas slippers, who seemed to know Jamal, let them through. Jamal motioned to her to follow him.

They made their way through the narrow wrought-iron gate, which squeaked when pulled, and Nadine followed Jamal into the inner courtyard.

The soft, wet moss under her shoes felt strangely comforting, as did the quiet of this place, enveloped in shadows and sagging, flowerless jacarandas, which soon would bloom with an explosion of purple and lavender flowers, the only remaining sign of changing seasons in Casablanca.

Jamal pushed open the front door, and there they were met by an equally enfolding and comforting darkness. They walked down the corridor, and in its half-light, Nadine noticed peeling paint on the walls and cracks in the linoleum. Once past the corridor, they opened another door and discovered a wide, bright space that seemed to be a waiting room. At its very end, a huge man was seated behind a desk. The man had muscles like burnt tires after a day of protests and gentle, sleepy eyes. The waiting room was empty at this hour of the night, but Nadine could hear, coming from down the hallway, the sounds of babies crying and of low voices conversing with each other.

The half-asleep, giant-like assistant behind the front desk grumbled that Nayla would be out to see them soon. Nadine and Jamal sat on one of the gray leatherette seats that, given the state of the place, must have been a donation to the center sometime in the past ten years. Sitting there, Nadine noticed doors lining the hallway leading from the waiting room. Each door seemed to be covered in bright colors.

Curious, she got up and walked down the hallway, and Jamal followed. The colors turned out to be joyful graffiti that must have been both sprayed and painted on. The only graffiti Nadine had ever seen before was on building exteriors. Close up, it had a different kind of undeniable power.

She stopped in front of each door, taking it all in, as did Jamal. At the top of each door was a sign that resembled the graffiti on the door: "Restroom," "Nursery," "Dormitory," "Infirmary," "Kitchen." Below each word was a vivid, exaggerated drawing to represent it. None of the rooms were ones Nadine was surprised to see in a women's center that cared for young mothers and their newborns. What surprised her were the words on three other doors farther down the hallway: "Classroom," "Music Room," "Book Club." She stared at these signs and the victorious graffiti below, unable to resist touching the colors, feeling their strength and vitality under her fingertips, and wondering at their presence in a place like this. Despite its peeling paint and used furniture, the center breathed permanence and safety. And determination.

"You've found the beating heart of our center," said a warm voice behind her.

Nadine turned around, and there stood a medium-height, athletic, young woman. She couldn't be more than thirty. The woman was smiling, a smile both vibrant and serene.

Nayla wasn't what Nadine had expected. She wore black converse sneakers, wide pants, a masculine shirt, and a black leather jacket. Her ears and nose were pierced, and her jet-black hair was cropped short in the back and hung long in the front. She looked more like a musician than the director of a women's center in Casablanca and a recognized advocate for women's rights in an Arab country. Though she looked so young, it didn't take long to see how tough and resilient she was. Nayla was a black belt judoka, and rumor had it she fought and scared off four men who had tried to assault her. She was already something of a legend.

So here was the source of this place's energy, Nadine realized. Here is the person who breathed her soul into the place, her vitality and her strength.

Jamal introduced them, and Nayla shook Nadine's hand before pulling her into a bear hug. Nadine felt the other woman's heat and power course through her. No one had held her in that way in years.

Nayla pulled away and pointed to the words on the doors.

"Not all the women who come to us can read or write. Some can, but most have few skills, or even hobbies. We use the power of music, art, graphic novels, and picture books to heal and help them make sense of things that don't make any."

"But that's not all they do here," said Jamal.

Nayla nodded.

"As soon as they can, we try to teach them a vocation so that they can start earning a living. This center is the only support system most of them have, even if it's only a temporary one, and as you see, funds are lacking. Our goal is that, when they leave, they can hold their heads high, have a way to be self-sufficient, be proud of their children and of being a mother. And our door always remains open to them, as much as we can, with our limited means."

Nayla spoke in a manner unlike anyone Nadine had ever met. She stirred together Casablanca-street Arabic, French and American-style English into her own personal mix of rough talk and kindness that touched Nadine in so many ways.

"But the truth is, many people only finance things that give them more power, status. And because most donors are men, and single mothers are considered a threat, centers like this will only ever barely survive. But we can't quit, right? One day, one day, it will be possible for women to have kids, or not, as they see fit, to have these kids recognized by the law, and have their own lives protected by the law. To have control of their lives and bodies," she added switching to English.

Nadine was beginning to feel out of place in this women's sanctuary. Too close, and too far, she kept thinking to herself. This girl was too strong. Her own daughter, Al, had that same fierceness, and it frightened her.

"Tell her about the art work," said Jamal.

"We're friends with a young girls' orphanage in the neighborhood. Actually, it's more like a real home than an orphanage, the way they treat the young women. Then they come here and draw their graffiti for us, and in exchange we give them free classes and group support sessions in the evening."

"Are you a social worker?"

"I'm a nurse, in fact."

She paused and smiled at Nadine, whose apprehension began to melt.

"So many of the women who come to us are in poor health. Their bodies have been carrying so much pain, scars they can't afford to tend to. Their bodies are bent and broken beyond their years. The body knows when it is abused, even if the mind denies it, or knows it doesn't have the luxury or the tools to heal it. That's why I built this center—to help women heal and do something for themselves and their children."

Nadine could barely hide her admiration or her envy of Nayla. She herself had given up her own pediatric practice, depriving others, and herself, of her hard-earned skills. And here was Nayla, trained as a nurse, whose oath was strong as steel.

"You do amazing work," she said, the pain in her chest easing.

Nayla nodded, simply.

"It's so little, not even close to enough."

"At least you don't give up," said Nadine.

Nayla's eyes shined.

"The woman who trained me—saved me actually—taught me that the dumber and meaner things get, the smarter and tougher you've got to be.

She glanced at Jamal and reflected for a moment.

"None of this would be possible without the work of others," continued Nayla, opening her palm toward him. "People like Jamal, who keep trying to tell the stories we're not allowed to tell. Who educate us, help change the mood on the street, shift public opinion. Some lawyers as well, doctors," she said with a little bow of her head to Nadine. "Not many, but they're here. And of course, young people. Casablanca's rising generation, it's a surprising one—unbelievably fierce, full of hope, doesn't take no for an answer. Iconoclastic and idealistic."

"Arrogant and impatient," Jamal laughed.

Nayla's eyes lit up with pleasure, and she laughed with him. These were old, close friends. Their deep ties made Nadine sense her own isolation and detachment.

Nayla turned to her.

"So, you're here to see one of the women we serve. Jamal told me who you are. I respect your decision to come here. I'm also surprised. Not many wives would do what you're doing."

"I'm not sure I understand," said Nadine.

Jamal and Nayla exchanged quick glances. Then Nayla changed the conversation.

"Let's go to my office. We'll be more comfortable there, and I want to get to know you better."

They followed Nayla down the narrow hallway.

———❊———

Nayla's office was a narrow room, packed with books, random mismatched armchairs collected from various second-hand sales or donations, and worn, yarn carpets. On the wall behind her desk hung a portrait of a curly-haired, bespectacled woman, holding in her wide, welcoming arms two very young children.

Nayla heated water and served them tea bags, cold milk, and cookies.

She shrugged, her eyes twinkling.

"Sorry I can't offer you more. But everyone says these are absolutely the best cheap tea and cookies they've ever had."

Nadine sipped the tea with milk, and the cookies. They tasted warm and spicy, sweet and strong. Actually, they were the best cheap tea and cookies she'd ever had. For the first time since she'd gotten to the center, she smiled. The lines on her face softened, her chest felt less tight.

"Well?" asked Nayla.

"The best I ever had," Nadine admitted.

Jamal hit the table with his open hand and roared.

Nayla laughed as well, joyfully, uninhibited.

"I'm part of a long line of ones who turn stone and ice into bread and fire. Like you, though you may have forgotten it." she said to Nadine. "And I'm protected by powerful women," she added, pointing upwards. "And the one whose name is on the Center's gate, do you remember who she is?"

Nadine's discomfort returned. She shifted in her chair.

"Yes. I believe I do. Fatima Zahra Al-Fihriya's sister."

Nayla nodded, so Nadine continued.

"Fatima Zahra built Al-Qarawiyyin in Fes, the first university in the world, in the ninth century. And her sister, Maryam, built the lesser known Andalus Mosque and Medersa."

"Lesser known but equally stunning," Nayla replied. "When you think that two North African women built the first universities in the world, two hundred years before Oxford and Bologna. I named my center for Maryam, the lesser known sister, the underdog, because they're the future."

She then pointed her thumb toward the woman in the portrait behind her.

"Of course you know Aicha Chenna, our country's very own mother to all single mothers, and to the children abandoned by the fathers, by the state. She never gave up on me. She lifted me up when I felt lower than dirt. She was a warrior. And my inspiration."

Nadine realized she was in an alien world, where the past, and the heroic, were transformed to fit the present in radical novelty, without fear or taboo.

Nayla leaned back.

"But enough."

Her eyes turned a steely gray.

"Mrs. Mesari, Nadine…before I take you to the young woman, let me make sure again. You're here to help this young mother and her child? No tricks? Otherwise, you're out of here."

Over the past day, Nadine had ricocheted from feelings of dryness, to burning, to heaviness, a constant upheaval leaving only a furious, raging heart. Her mouth was dry, and her words came out in a voice that was not quite hers, but that may well have been her actual voice.

"I need to know something first."

Nayla looked at her warily.

"What do you need to know?"

"Is the woman in your care named Ghalia Ait Iddin? And is her child called Noor?"

Nayla nodded, but didn't interrupt.

"And is this little boy, this Noor, is he the son of Kamal Mesari, my husband?"

Nayla nodded again.

All turned quiet in the broken-down office with the used furniture and the cheap tea and cookies. All seemed to go quiet in the center, in the street, in the neighborhood, in the city. The quiet was so quiet that Nadine knew it came from within her, not from the world around her.

"Go on. Don't stop there," Jamal said, breaking the silence, his voice steady and clear, as though something more than sympathy for Nadine forced him to speak.

"Ask if the mother is okay. Ask how this woman feels after having her trust broken by an employer, someone powerful who should have kept to himself. Ask how the little boy is. If he's feeding, if he's sleeping, if he has nightmares, if he knows what's coming next. What is it like to be them?"

But all Nadine could imagine was this woman with her husband, behind her back, in her own home. The perversity, she thought, the arrogance. How they must have laughed at her. Her anger burst out with a hiss.

"What's happening here? What kind of place is this? I'm the victim here. She went with a man who wasn't hers. She dreamed of him being hers. She dreamed of being me, of erasing me. That child, he's the consequence of her ambition, of the game she chose to play. Why did I come here? To be abused again? To be manipulated and blamed for actions that aren't my doing? You're not so different from him, from men like him, Jamal, even though you denounce them. But she's to blame, more than he is. She played and she lost."

Nadine stopped.

She had revealed more of herself to these two strangers than she had to the people closest to her. They knew more of what lay in her heart than the man who shared her life. And why should they be benevolent toward her? They were the types of people who helped the weak, helped those in need of help, not someone apparently like herself—one of the uncaring enablers, the ones who refuse to see or change.

But to her surprise, Nayla smiled gently.

"You know, we're not so different, you and I, even if we come from worlds apart. We're stuck in this together, this old story, our legacy. Women's bodies enslaved in castles and fortresses, the *kasbahs* and *ksars* of North Africa, to serve in the masters' homes, to raise the children, serve the masters' needs. This old story that's still with us in our customs, our treatment of women and children, our unchanging caste system of wealth and power. It still runs in our veins, shapes our gaze, our desires. How can we make peace with it without understanding the roles we've been made to play?"

Nayla wrapped her arms around her body in a surprisingly vulnerable, protective way, her leather jacket creaking as she did.

"When I was twenty, I was forced to give up my baby. The father wouldn't come through for us. My family were poor. So my parents took away my baby, threw me out. I've never found out what happened to her, she must be dead. I pray she's dead, it's best for her. And this woman," she said pointing to the portrait of Aicha Chenna above her desk, "she took me in, trained me, helped me."

She thought for a moment.

"We're all trapped in this, deformed by it. But then we victimize others, right? The master becomes brutal, heartless, arrogant, but also, paranoid, fearful, perverse. He claims something that's not his, is haunted at night by the fear of being killed in his sleep for taking what belongs to someone else. And the ones on the bottom, we learn to become servile, submissive, full of doubt and self-loathing. Two sides, unable to break free. Most often that means the master—or his son—taking advantage of the slave girl, servant, these days the housekeeper, living in their midst."

She turned to Jamal, including him in her impassioned rant.

"It's like they know it's okay, instinctively, like it's their birthright, their rite of passage. Women taken at will have always been called names—witch, whore, seductress. The ones with power put their desire in her. Then they say she's the one with the great, endless appetite. She's the one with the red lips and round hips and the smooth, golden skin, the strength and the fire that ensnares and seduces. And they try to take away even that power from her. They're the ones responsible for the greatest evils. The enslaved are to blame."

For a moment, Nadine thought she saw black flames and serpents entwined in Nayla's hair, a Medusa that you shouldn't cross lest she turn you into stone, and Jamal was no journalist at all, but a giant with a saber in his hand, ready for battle.

She closed her eyes, and when she opened them again, Nayla was her old self, in her sneakers and oversized clothes, and Jamal, thick-set, weathered, and unflinching.

Nadine gathered her thoughts.

"Even if a lot of what you say is true, are they only victims? Don't housekeepers sometimes seduce their employers?"

"Of course, but that is not the case with Ghalia and…your husband," Jamal said, as gently as he could. "It isn't what you think, Nadine. It's not a love story, it's not about guile and seduction, even though he may have tried to persuade you it is. It's about violence."

"That's a lie."

"Think about it. Imagine a situation where your employer has almost full power over you. And that his wife, his family, his colleagues, everyone around him, always believes that the man is the victim, the weak one, the one who's seduced. Wouldn't that frighten you? Wouldn't you try to escape, to regain your freedom? But let's go. If you're ready to hear it, Ghalia will tell you herself."

Jamal noticed tears in her eyes. He paused and leaned toward her.

"You are brave, Nadine," he said gently. "Braver than you think. And kind, as only brave people can be. You've known this and thought about it for a long time now. Otherwise you wouldn't be here with us. Ask yourself the right questions. In your heart, you know the answers."

Nadine let the tears roll down her cheeks.

"Jamal, leave us a minute first," asked Nayla.

Jamal left the room.

---

Nayla turned to Nadine.

"He can be harsh, but it's only on the outside. We've fought side-by-side for ten years. But he's dedicated fifty years of his life to changing all this, to pushing for more just laws. And what he's been through, it's hardened him."

"He only sees one side of the story."

"Maybe. Who doesn't sometimes? But what he doesn't tell people is that he was one of these kids he's trying to save."

"What do you mean?"

"It was another era, over sixty years ago. His mother had him while she was still living with her father, his grandfather. She had him out of wedlock. His grandfather kept him, but the mother disappeared. No one ever found her or heard from her again."

"What happened to her?"

"Don't know. Jamal tried to find her, but he never could. He believes she was killed by her relatives and buried near their village."

Nadine sat still.

"In every abandoned child, he sees himself. And it's a miracle it has made him the person he is, and not broken him."

"And you, Nayla?"

"Me? Sure, I see my child, the one I never really held in my arms, in every child. I celebrate every life saved, even if there aren't that many. And I try not to break with each loss. The losses are great, but we have to survive them."

Nadine's mind was made up. She got up, and Nayla stood as well.

"All right, let's go to them," said Nadine.

Nayla hugged Nadine firmly in her arms. Then she opened the door and called to Jamal. He came back into the office and looked at Nadine, and a slow, sheepish smile, of relief, of hope, lit his face.

# 8
# The Window

Nadine and Jamal followed Nayla down the softly lit hallway toward the part of the building that sheltered the mothers and their newborns. Nadine was reminded of how, after the death of her son, she'd thought of adopting a child, a little boy, perhaps. But Kamal and his mother wouldn't hear of it.

They continued down the hall to a door on the left.

"Ghalia is alone in a room, for the time being," Nayla explained. "Her little one is weak."

She knocked but got no answer. Nayla knocked again. She waited, then opened the door and turned on the light.

"They're gone."

The room was empty. The cot had been overturned, and a small pile of clothes remained in the drawer.

"Why would they leave?" Nayla said to Nadine, despair in her voice. "Why didn't anyone see them leave?"

Jamal started searching the room, flipping over the covers, looking under the bed, peering at dirty footprints covering a corner of the carpet, opening and closing the single window that faced onto the courtyard, not far below them. When he was done, he turned to Nayla.

"They left through the window. There was a struggle. She didn't go willingly. At first. Who else but you and I knew they were here?"

"No one. I told Ghalia very clearly that, for now, for her own safety, she couldn't tell anyone where she was."

Nayla stopped to think. Then she phoned the gentle muscle-man receptionist, who answered with sleep still filling his mouth.

"Jaafar, did anyone come through here this afternoon or this evening? Did you hear any unusual sounds?"

From Nayla's expression, it was clear that he hadn't seen or heard anything. It was as if a ghost had come in and taken the woman and her child away.

"Come," she said, "we must hurry. We need to talk to the guard. It's not possible he didn't see anyone come through. He sees everything."

---

They followed her out of the center, onto the paved pathway to the small garden in the front. By the gate stood the old man dressed in a brown wool djellaba, thick socks, and black-and-white Adidas sandals. He steadied himself with a long stick he gripped, and he was busy spitting dried sunflower seed shells out of his toothless mouth. He seemed content, at ease, his white-blue gaze turned more toward the stars than the street.

"Hadj Mohand," Nayla said interrupting his star-gazing and sunflower shell spitting. "In the past two hours, have you seen anyone come in?"

Hadj Mohand looked at her, startled, but quickly shook his head.

"No, Nayla. No one came through here. Nothing and no one comes through without me noticing. The wind comes through, I see it, I hear it. The only people who came through this evening are Jamal and his friend here."

He sank his weight more heavily onto the stick in his hand, still chewing the last sunflower seeds.

"Hadj Mohand, think, please. Anyone. Men running errands, men who said they had an appointment, carrying goods for the Center."

Hadj Mohand shook his head, saddened that he wasn't able to give her a satisfying answer, and slightly worried that he missed something very important. He closed his eyes and tried to remember the late afternoon and early evening hours.

It was hard to remember anything, because when he wasn't spitting dried sunflower shells, he was rolling his hashish and smoking it under the pungent Jasmine tree, hopeful that the earthy smell of his cigarette would blur with the tree's divine flower scent.

But then it came to him, as through a mist, blurred and hazy.

He shook his head once more, averting his gaze in embarrassment and perhaps also in fear, for he too had seen Nayla's hair turn black flame and coiling serpent.

"There is one thing, Nayla. But it's nothing, not what you're looking for. Not men. At least not more than one…"

"Tell me, Hadj Mohand. You have nothing to fear, but a young woman and her baby—their lives may be at stake."

The old security guard sighed, looked at the stars one last time.

"Listen, like I said, it's probably nothing. Two men, in their middle years I would say, came at around seven this evening. They seemed exhausted and hungry. They had a gardener's wheelbarrow and a large hemp bag, filled with leaves and grass, I'd say, not middle aged. Old men, harmless…

They said they gardened the street outside the center but that they were very tired and had nowhere to rest, and could they please just rest for a little against the tree, or anywhere in the garden. I led them toward the bench against the wall on the other side of the courtyard, by the windows of our residents. And that was that. I did God's work."

"Did you see them leave?"

Hadj Mohand looked even more embarrassed and was getting agitated.

"How should I know? Two tired, old, harmless drifters, don't I have more important things to look out for? They couldn't have gotten inside from there. I would've seen them. Haven't you trusted me all these years, without regret?"

Despite the anger in his voice, there was despair in his eyes.

Jamal went quickly to the bench Hadj Mohand had described. It was almost directly beneath Ghalia's window.

"It wouldn't have been difficult for the men to climb up the wall and bring Ghalia and the child down with them," he said as he walked back to them.

"But who are these men and how did they know where to find her?" Nadine asked.

Nadine looked up at the window. Though it was a short jump down, it would still be hard to get a woman and her child down from there.

"Why didn't she scream? Why didn't she call for help?" she said. "Ghalia's a brave girl, strong and willful. She wouldn't just agree to go, without resisting, with her child, after all that she went through to reach safety."

Nayla and Jamal looked at her.

"Are you saying she may have known the two men?" asked Jamal.

"Yes."

"How would they have known she was here?"

Nadine thought of the wedding picture, proudly displayed in the Ait Iddin's home, of the too young bride with the short, unruly hair, which must be long by now.

"I believe Ghalia would have told her sister. And these men could have gotten the information from the sister," said Nadine.

"Why would she betray her own sister?" asked Nayla. "Ghalia told me how close they were. It was the person she was closest to in the family. It doesn't make sense."

"Maybe Ghalia's sister didn't betray her," Nadine replied. "Maybe her sister was forced to give up the information, was threatened. Maybe these men threatened the family."

"Do you have an idea who these men are?" Nayla persisted.

"They could have been in disguise. And it got them past poor Hadj Mohand's failing eyes," said Jamal.

"We need to find out where she was taken," Nadine said.

Jamal looked at Nadine and smiled at the change that he saw in her in just the few hours he had known her.

When she came into his office, she had seemed almost old. Her hair was in a low ponytail, her pale green eyes were a washed-up gray, like the seaside before a storm. She didn't stand straight and constantly averted her gaze, rubbing her hands together as if trying to take comfort where none could be found. She seemed to have lost a piece of herself a long time ago, and yet didn't know what she had lost.

Now, her hair shone bright, like silver and gold entwined, there was a bold light in her green eyes, and she stood straight, perhaps because she remembered that she was still youthful and could hold her own. How quickly an individual could light up with the hope of action, Jamal thought, or have the light taken from them with the threat of despair.

"What do you suggest?" he asked.

"We need to find Ghalia's sister and have her tell us what she knows. She's our only hope," said Nadine.

"Why would she help us?" Jamal asked.

"When I was at the Ait Iddins' this morning, there was a portrait of the sister and her new husband. She looked no older than fifteen. The groom seemed to be in his fifties, if not older, a friend of the father's. They may have married her off when they found out about Ghalia's condition. If she was married by force, she may want to help us."

"She'd never dare help us," said Jamal. "Do you know how these child brides live? What's done to them?"

"Defiance is still possible," said Nadine, her temper rising a little.

"Is it?"

Nayla interrupted.

"If the Ait Iddins feel that their honor has been damaged by Ghalia and the baby, they could be trying to save their reputation by marrying their young daughter to the highest bidder, a man who's established. That's an alliance with a more powerful family, and hope that the sister will grow up and forget what was done to her. They may have seemed like modern city dwellers to you, Nadine, with their jobs and their apartment. But don't be fooled: old ways can be transformed in the city, but they die hard."

Jamal put a hand on Nayla's arm.

"Wait, we may be onto something. Nadine, from meeting the Ait Iddins, do you actually think this young girl would go against the people who own her, would risk her life, to help us?"

"I do," Nadine replied. "You said it yourself, she's not free. But that doesn't mean she doesn't want to be, that she wouldn't do this for her sister. That she's broken."

Nayla nodded.

"It's a risk," Nayla said. "Things could get even more out of control. But it's worth a try. Jamal, please call the mother. Threaten her with another article, if you have to."

Jamal called Lamis Ait Iddin's cell phone.

...

"Mrs. Ait Iddin, this is Jamal Bidoun…Yes, the journalist who wrote about your daughter. I'm sorry to have to tell you this, but your daughter, perhaps both your daughters, and a child—your grandchild—are in danger. I need your younger daughter's number and address…

"I'm not threatening you, Madam, just telling you the facts…No, I won't tell your husband, and I swear it won't be in the newspapers…I'll be discreet."

Jamal listened intently and carefully wrote down the information Lamis gave him.

"Thank you very much, Mrs. Ait Iddin."

He hung up and turned to Nadine and Nayla.

"Here's the daughter's number and address. The mother seems in on it," he said handing it to Nadine.

"It's in the *Centre-Ville*—eleven Rue Pierre Malard," he said. "Not far from the central market, behind Derb Omar merchants' neighborhood."

# Part III

# 9
# City Streets

*That evening*

Darkness had swallowed the city. The dense streets were emptied of cars, trucks, taxis, and outstretched hands. The streetlights shed dim light and trembling shadows on the streets, sidewalks, and building walls below and around them. The paper-thin whiteness of the city's buildings contrasted with the surrounding shade and deep fissures apparent on almost every façade.

At night, the city transformed into another beast altogether. And yet, Nadine found it to be more alive, more truthful than during the day. It revealed its true self: a white exterior, cold and unmoving, which barely pretended to hide the cracks that ran through the streets, buildings, gardens, the people themselves.

Kamal had once told her, when he was still trying to impress her, that Casablanca was a city dedicated to the night. It was called the white city; but it was built, during the French Protectorate, for the Europeans' pleasure. It became alive at night—with its bars, whorehouses, restaurants, and nightclubs that filled up with prostitutes, local Europeans, and their Moroccan cronies and collaborators. It was a new city, industrial and mercantile during the day, wild and inebriated at night. When the French left, most of the night places closed. But the hardcore, phantasmagoric, breathless pace of the city remained, for those who knew how to look in its cracks and darkness.

Nadine drove Nayla and Jamal down the empty streets, ran red lights, and crossed empty boulevards that made them feel like ghosts. During the day, it takes close to an hour to get from the *Quartier des Hôpitaux* to the *Centre-Ville*. But now they brushed through its expanse in less than fifteen minutes, painting the city with their receding lights. Speeding through its unknowable spaces, they dared believe there was beauty within, and much-desired salvation.

They soon reached the Rue Pierre Malard. It was a dark street with formidable buildings whose style combined Art Deco with Moorish architecture to create something foreboding and otherworldly. At their very top, the buildings seemed to lean and sway into the void; and where once fashionable penthouses overlooked the city horizon, now were broken-down bay windows and wooden carcasses barely holding together. Elegant French couples of the Protectorate Era had been replaced by innumerable Moroccan squatters, tied together by blood, addiction, or circumstance. Nadine stared at these chic, decrepit mid-rises and thought of the lesson in architecture her husband would surely give them, the swooping, brittle changes he would make to the facades, the layouts, and most importantly, to the inhabitants.

---

They parked the car on a side street that curled in the night toward the white arcades and green *azulejos*, the tiles of the

*Marché Central.* It would have been, on any other day, a stroll through a Casablanca that no longer was and had never been. An architect's dream, a colonial fantasy of colorful characters and beautifully laid-out fish, oysters, sea urchins, clams, mussels on crushed ice, red and white meats slowly swaying from rounded steel hooks; fruit and vegetable stalls spread out in a myriad of colors, textures, and scents; a constant bustle and the cheerful, hardened voices of merchants, vendors, butchers, and fishmongers.

And at the back of the market, a tree-shaded street where antique dealers peddled their wares, swearing to the high heavens that they were real, genuine, though not many people knew or could tell the difference. Beside them, rare book dealers sitting on the ground beside their high-stacked books and paraphernalia dating from the French Protectorate and World War II, selling poetry by Rimbaud, novels by Victor Hugo, impossible-to-find editions of encyclopedias, bizarre medical dictionaries, and maps scaled, it is true, by the first Arab cartographer, Al Idrissi himself, "Yes sir, yes little lady, in the twelfth century, before any European cartographer knew the world was even round," quipped the bookseller; along with extinct tourist brochures, and Aeropostale posters. And finally, advertisements of chocolate powder with a smiling black face, large red lips, and bulging white eyes on a yellow background; licorice in the shapes of feathered Native Americans; small monkeys, little black people, imitations of Delacroix paintings of Arab merchants praying away from Mecca, sprawled here and there on the sandy road, and of odalisques beckoning the weary traveler's lurid gaze—paintings that were themselves orientalist fantasies of a misunderstood place.

All the exotic paraphernalia of the East that the French had invented and constructed, gleefully and carelessly, and showcased in this incomparable space that was the *Marché Central*. A souk that the *Casablancais* had reclaimed as their own, finding a common destiny to a people of migrants, to a population that came from every corner of the kingdom and that took upon itself to create something new, even if artificial, impossible and detached from history. A space now doomed to destruction by a more forward looking urban planning division, condemning this decades old circus to barren streets without homes.

———※※———

Nadine had heard of the bicycle city tours that offered a stroll to and through the *Marché Central* and had promised herself, when times were better, to share this experience with Al, but only now remembered that promise.

She had herself once walked its streets, caressed its books, ate its oysters fresh from their shells, on tiptoe by the central fish stall held in place by an intimidating female fishmonger by the name of Khadija, and drank the peculiar energy that throbbed through Casablanca's *Marché Central*.

The energy harnessed from being close to many faces of despair and the down and out, to an aimless, urban kaleidoscope, started to hit Nadine. It was a cinema of sorts, where all were both actors and spectators. It was a city that didn't allow for a tranquil life, that shook you regularly throughout your existence, no matter who you were, for no one here, not even the most powerful, were safe from harm and the arbitrary hand of destiny.

They were on the other, less known façade of the *Marché Central*. Its phantasmagoric bustle was a thing of the day. At night, it was deserted, patrolled by cops, but only on its outskirts, and only the most daring, or the most desperate, would venture to spend the night within its walls, in whose shade hid the city's cutthroats, sometimes as young as ten, and, some whispered, and some witnessed, the human ghosts and djinns that had been banished from paradise.

Perpendicular to the Rue Pierre Malard, and extending toward the more hilly, peaceful residential neighborhood of Polo, was the merchants' market of Derb Omar, as old as the city itself and equally filled with immigrants who hailed from other, more ancient but less vibrant urban centers—from Fes and Rabat, from Marrakesh and Agadir, from Taroudant, Guelmim, from Tangiers, Tetouan, Oujda, and Nador, from the saintly city of Bejaad and the rebel city of Chaouen; from the center, the east, the south and from the north. They bartered, negotiated, and sold the wares they had brought from Egypt, Spain, England, and from as far away as China and India. Silver, sari cloth, plastic bowls and cups, toys, carpets and textiles, cotton and kitchenware.

Great fortunes hid in its narrow alleys, a know-how that didn't always translate into the global Internet age, a firm rejection of school, and a diehard belief that barter was gold and that tireless work, a honey tongue, and a promise honored were worth more than books and degrees. A pool of talent and mercantile skill as ancient as the Mediterranean traders themselves, as sophisticated as the Phoenicians and the desert caravans that linked Timbuktu to the Silk Road. A market from whence many families she knew had harnessed their wealth and their reputation, pretending they were modern, hiding their connections to, and love of, a way of doing business that was quickly being taken away from them. Now quiet, its stalls were dark under the lowered metal rollers.

Nadine, Nayla, and Jamil stood in the dark street with the single flickering lamp post, their eyes adjusting to its feeble light, struggling to find the building number that had been given them by Lamis Ait Iddin.

# 10
# Swaying Building

Minutes passed before they realized that the imposing, rundown building in front of them was the very place they were looking for. It was a building that spoke of past wealth and long-gone residents. It was one of those buildings, like many in the city, where rent control and complex inheritance laws thwarted any concerted effort at improvement or a lucrative sale. Half of the building appeared vacant and the other half bursting at the seams from all the wooden frames and cement added to hold the facade in place.

"Is this it? It seems empty," said Nadine.

"It looks like many of these apartments are sweatshops," said Jamal. "But some are still occupied."

"I'm surprised that an immigrant to Belgium, who has found work in Europe, would live in a place like this," she said.

"It's his mother's apartment," he answered and handed her the address.

Nadine stared at the piece of paper in her hands. She checked the address over and over again, looking up at the commanding building akin to a slum. It seemed as if a spider's web was being woven in front of her, for her. She wondered what she was walking into, all the difficulties of life when simplicity and security aren't possible, when choices darken and cracks and chasms deepen under the feet.

She breathed.

The city smells were strong. During the day, car fumes and coal-fed street foods rose through the air, hot and strong. At night, here in the heart of the city, the scents had turned cold, stale, the oil shone on the greasy pavements, the polluting heat turned into a hard, fatal toxicity. There was something wrong with this place. Even the cockroaches and the rats lurked in fear. She felt like running away, disappearing into the night. But she remembered something she had almost forgotten. She was tough.

"Third floor, apartment thirty-one," said Nadine. "It's almost dawn, we need to hurry."

⸻ ❖ ⸻

The building's wrought-iron front door was covered with rust. Its stained glass had been replaced by roughly planked sheets of wood.

They entered.

The black-and-white marble floor still showed signs of past glory, despite the cracks, dust, and dirt. People had come and gone, their opulence and arrogance forgotten, their feet barely leaving a mark in the dimly lit, broken-down foyer. The walls leaked through the pink granite, now brown, and torn in places.

Unsurprisingly, the elevator was broken, so they took the stairs, using their phone flashlights to light their way. The first two floors seemed like an abandoned building, if it weren't for the occasional lights that appeared down the hallways from beneath closed doors on either side.

The third floor seemed more occupied than the first two. Monotonous buzzing sounds reached the hallway from kitchen appliances or the TV. From behind some doors came the sounds of running water, of faucets being shut off.

In front of apartment thirty-one, they stopped. They were relieved to see light from beneath the doorway and hear slow, buzzing sounds coming from inside. Hopefully, they soon would be with Ghalia and her child and know if they were okay, know if this wild chase hadn't been in vain. But the sounds were perhaps a little too mundane, the light slightly too soft, the normalcy of a late Casablanca evening perhaps too casual.

Nadine rang the doorbell, and they waited. No one came to the door.

So Jamal knocked.

They waited.

Finally, the lock tumbled, and the door was pulled ajar.

An elderly woman, heavyset, turban wound around her head, flowery nightgown that grazed the floor, stood in front of them, blocking the door frame. She stared at them, her mouth a thin line under her wrinkled cheeks and thick chin.

"Who are you? What do you want?"

Jamal replied in his most courteous voice, the one he used to interview frightened witnesses, or criminals posing as victims.

"Madam, we're looking for a young woman—Yasmina Ait Iddin. We were told we'd find her here, under your good care."

The woman's chest heaved.

"What do you want with her?"

"Just to ask her a few questions."

"At this hour?"

"It's about her sister."

"Yasmina doesn't have a sister."

"And a little boy."

"You have the wrong people."

"It's a serious matter, Madam, to take the law into your own hands."

"What do you want with this Yasmina?"

"I suggest you let us in and let us talk to Yasmina. Before things get worse—very quickly. We just need to see if the young woman and her child are okay."

"Who are you?"

"Friends of the young woman."

"I'm alone in the house. I don't know these people."

"That's strange. It was Yasmina's mother herself, Mrs. Ait Iddin, who gave us your address. She said that Yasmina's your daughter-in-law, that she's living here with you while your son, her newly betrothed, is back in Belgium. Is that correct?"

"You're doing the devil's work, Mister, and at dawn, disturbing my prayers, waking up the angels."

"We mean no harm, I promise you. We only need to make sure everyone is okay. Better us than the police, isn't that right, Mrs…?"

"Mrs. Fareeda Boujloud," she said.

She peered closely at the three strangers standing in front of her. At last, she opened the door and let them in.

"You may come in, but I'm telling you, there's no one here."

"Thank you, Mrs. Boujloud," Jamal said, tipping his head a little, as though he were wearing a hat.

———— ❦ ————

The layout was typical of a thirties apartment. A square foyer, glass doors that led into a living-room and dining-room, a long hallway to the right where the bedrooms and bathroom would be, and, next to the dining room, a kitchen. The apartment was dark and unkept. Dust rose in the half gloom and spiderwebs covered corners and doorways.

Fareeda Boujloud led them into the living room but didn't offer them a seat.

"As you can see, the place is empty. It's just me. It's true that my son left his bride in my care so he could go back to Brussels to work. He wanted her to be in good hands until he could come for her. And for me. It's been his dream, to bring me to Europe in the best way, well-off and respected. He's a good son. He didn't even want to get married. He said women get spoiled in Belgium. But I convinced him. You see, he needs a woman, a wife. What will the neighbors think?"

"Where is Yasmina, Mrs. Boujloud, if she's not here?" Jamal asked.

"My son is a good man. A man of morals and religion. But he was naive. He married this young girl. They sang her praises, and he believed them. He believed she was pure and good. He believed she would be obedient and hard-working. That she was the woman he was looking for. But I took one look at her, and I knew. I knew what she was hiding behind her coy exterior. I'm an old woman. I told my son over and over not to marry just anyone, that he deserved the purest of women—strong, silent, hard-working, who would do his bidding and respect her elders. But one look at her and he stopped listening. The devil's work, I tell you."

"So you don't approve of your son's choice of bride," said Jamal curtly.

"She's a bad apple. Only women can see through other women. Men see, God forgive these base words, only with one part of their bodies, even my own son. At his age, a mature man in his late fifties, he fell into her trap."

She waited for a reaction, but none came, not even an encouraging nod. She lowered her voice.

"My son asked me to take her in, after he married her. I did. I was kind to her. But she wasn't clean."

Jamal lowered his voice, as well.

"I'm sorry Mrs. Boujloud. I don't understand what that means."

"Of course you don't. They do," she said waving her hand toward the two women standing in front of her, who weren't at all helping her get her point across.

"She wasn't pure. Men had touched her before. She was used."

Her three guests were cold as ice, standing in her living room. They might as well have been made of stone.

"Look, she's only sixteen, and already! Thank God my son isn't that stupid. He left her here with me when he found out she wasn't clean. He's not coming back for her, that's for sure."

"Is he gone?"

"Back to Brussels. Yes, sir. He's done now with that little whore. But it's the sister's fault, let me tell you."

"The sister? I thought you said she didn't have a sister?"

Fareeda Boujloud turned red.

"No. I won't dirty my mouth with words about that whore…"

Realizing her mistake, the old woman stopped. She pretended she couldn't breathe.

"I'm an old woman. Worked hard all my life. I don't know anything. Just what I heard."

"Tell us what you heard, Madam. Don't be afraid. It's all for the best," Jamal reassured her.

The words flowed from her mouth.

"She has an older sister. Ghalia, *the Precious One*. With a name like that, what did they expect? She was the pride of the family. An arrogant little thing, thought she was better than you because she had the looks and the brains. But that's not enough, is it? Being Godly, being respectful, obedient, that's how you tell a good woman from a bad one."

She chuckled, a deep, guttural sound, scratched her back, tried to catch her breath.

"She got herself into some trouble. When one apple rots, the entire lot rots along with it."

"Mrs. Boujloud, for any woman, there is justice, if the right person steps forward. Even for the righteous woman, such as yourself, there could be consequences, enemies to be found, debts to be paid," Jamal cautioned her.

"Don't threaten me. I have nothing to do with any of that."

"We're sure you don't," said Nayla. "But if you don't tell us where Yasmina and her sister are, we'll leave you no rest, and we won't be the only ones stepping through that door, peeking into your life, into your son's business in Brussels, into the fact he married a sixteen-year-old. We'll find lawyers here and in Brussels who will hunt your son down. You know those Northerners, don't you? You know they don't like Arabs who mistreat women, who marry little girls, you know they could find dirt in your son's past…"

Fareeda looked at them, her deep-sunk, cunning eyes gauging the danger she was in.

"My son is a decent, honorable, faithful man. He's not to blame."

"Who is, I wonder?" Nadine whispered, almost to herself.

These were the first words she had spoken since they came in.

"Where's Yasmina, Mrs. Boujloud?" she asked.

Fareeda shuffled, then sat up with difficulty.

"I need you to understand that this…Yasmina isn't who she says she is. I'll take you to her, but she's evil, she's dirty. Better you leave right now and not think about her, her sister, or that…But I see you insist. I'm a God-fearing woman, a good woman. I see evil and I root it out. That's what I've done my entire life, my life's work. My son, he knows, he's always looked up to me, respected my opinion."

Jamal lowered his head, took off his fogged up glasses, breathed on them, and began slowly wiping them clean.

"Of course, Mrs. Boujloud. We can see that. We understand your concerns. Don't worry. We just want to talk to Yasmina. We understand everything," he said.

He looked at Nayla and Nadine, who also nodded.

"I'll need some compensation, you see. This young girl, she washed and cleaned the house. What will I do now, all alone? An old woman…"

Nadine quickly looked into her bag, took out a two-hundred dirham bill.

"Will this do?"

Fareeda Boujloud sighed, her hands, like claws, around the bill.

"This will barely get me through the week…good deeds will always be rewarded, especially toward the old and helpless."

Nadine took out another bill, a one-hundred dirham bill, her face closed, and her hand cold. "This is it. Now show us the girl," she insisted.

Fareeda Boujloud chuckled again, that same bottomless, guttural sound. She was, Nadine realized, a terrifying woman, the kind known to roast and eat children in fairytales.

They followed her down the hallway. The air was cold and dank, and Nadine found it hard to breathe, as though she were outside in a dark alleyway. Behind the damp chill, she could smell another scent. An odor both familiar and foreign, one that would rise and cling and reveal something unforgivable about the world: the hallway smelled of rot. Was she the only one who noticed it? It was more than just a smell. It had a large, heaving body, a distinctive sickly sweetness that reminded her of male cologne over dirty skin, of dirty fingernails and unwashed hair, of deeds done in the dark and senseless cruelty.

When she reached the far end of the hallway, Fareeda Boujloud stopped and stood in front of a door. It was a small door, almost a trapdoor, with a double lock. She took keys out of her pocket, and as she pushed open the door, she gave them a final warning.

"Don't be fooled by this woman. She's filth. Do as you please. But then I want you all out of my house."

# 11
## Brown Door

As Fareeda Boujloud turned and walked back down the hallway, Nayla fought off the fury raging inside her. *"How easy it would be to plunge my knife into her heart,"* she growled to herself as she stood in front of the brown door with Jamal and Nadine. They had kept their thoughts, their words, even their breath to themselves this entire time. They had instinctively feared this woman's rough, volatile nature, and they had kept quiet, like a music box refusing to play after being wound up tight.

They went inside.

It was a small, narrow room, more like a cupboard.

Jamal turned on the light.

A young girl lay on a mattress on the floor. In one hand, she clenched an object. She was very quiet and didn't even seem to be breathing. The smell inside the room was strong, unclean, and had that same rotten scent Nadine smelled in the hallway.

Yasmina looked up at them. She curled up in fear, brought her knees to her chest. Nayla went to her, sat next to her, touched her hands gently.

"Don't worry, child. We came to get you out of here. We're friends of your sister."

Yasmina started crying, silently and uncontrollably.

"Come with us, child. You're safe now. Don't be scared."

She looked up at them, suddenly red in the face, a trace of fire in her black eyes.

"Oh, I'm not scared, you know. That old hag can do whatever she wants with me. She won't break me. She can die trying."

"That's right. She almost did die trying. But don't worry, we'll call the police as soon as we get you and your sister out of here," said Nayla.

"The police? They just eat poor people. They won't do anything to her. She has her ways out."

"Oh, they will," said Jamal. "This is a real set-up that woman has here. And if she wants to get rid of them, she'll have to pay them—a lot of money, and even then…"

"Her son isn't coming back, Yasmina," said Nadine. "Did you know that your husband is gone?" asked Nadine.

Nadine looked at Yasmina's thin frame and her dirty, straggly hair. Her fingers were long and delicate, like those of an artist or a musician. She almost had been turned into a waif, if it weren't for the black fire in her eyes.

Nadine recognized the object Yasmina had in her hand. It was a simple, hand-made motor, and she had seen it before. She remembered seeing it in Zahra's room one day, when she went down there. She rarely went to the housekeepers' quarters. Perhaps she was ashamed to see how people in her own house lived. But occasionally she would go down to find out if anything was needed or if some repair had to be done.

This time, looking around the rooms, she had found this motor on Jeanne's bed. She'd asked what it was, and Jeanne said it was a hobby of hers, making devices out of little pieces of junk that came her way. How did Yasmina get it?...Had the ties between Ghalia and Jeanne been stronger than she'd thought?

She wondered what Jeanne knew, what she had seen. Nadine's house was a house of lies and secrets. It was a house of whispered thoughts and unforgivable doings, a house divided in two: the ones with and the ones without. But she no longer knew where she herself belonged. How had she not seen it more clearly? Her daughter had.

"He isn't my husband," said Yasmina, bringing Nadine back from her thoughts. "The law can say he is, but what does the law know?"

"You may be right," said Nayla. "He may not be your legal husband, at least not in Belgium. We'll find out. But first, come, we need to get you out of here, get some warm food in you. And find your sister."

Nayla noticed Yasmina staring at her leather jacket. She smiled, took it off, and put it on the girl's shoulders

"You look tougher already. No one will mess with you now."

Yasmina grinned and looked at Nayla with awe. Nadine wondered if Yasmina too had never met one like her before, if she too was given wings and dreams just by looking at Nayla.

───※❈※───

They walked out of the room and across the hallway. Again, Nadine noticed that sickly sweet, pungent smell, like over-dried prunes, aging oranges, rotting apples. When they reached the doorway to the living-room, Fareeda Boujloud was standing there, her large frame and wrinkled arms and face boldly in the way.

"Where are you taking her?" she demanded.

"Madam, that is no longer your concern," said Jamal.

"She's my daughter-in-law. She's mine. I have a right to know."

"Tell your son that if he ever tries to reclaim Yasmina as his wife, we'll inform the Belgian police that they have a case of bigamy," said Nayla.

"You have no proof of that."

"I heard him speak to his wife and kids," said Yasmina, surprising them all.

Fareeda Boujloud began shaking.

"You lying piece of trash…"

"He has a wife, but he said she's been made dirty by Europe. He's only keeping her until we have kids, then he'll get rid of her."

"You filthy, stupid…"

"Oh, you didn't know, did you? Why do you think you're still here? Why do you think he doesn't come anymore? He's left you behind, the horror of you behind. He'll only come back for me. But I won't be here anymore. And I wish death upon you both."

Nadine put her hand on the young girl's arm.

"That's enough, child. Come, it's time we leave all this. It's time to go."

———

Fareeda Boujloud had always destroyed all those who had ever approached her, and there was no one left. None could match up to her singular moral code—a code that saw all women as whores and all men as victims, a code that sunk its roots in hatred of the human race and had bloomed in the darkness of a mind so strong and opaque that none had ever dared question it or confront it. All either fled or were crushed by it.

Fareeda was not one to lose a battle without a fight, without distilling poison or perverting a victory. She pressed herself against the door, blocking the exit. Fifty years of silence and slow rumination poured through her mind like acid.

All Yasmina had to do was to obey her. That was the way of the *tamghert*, the women. They had a code. You obeyed your elders until it was your turn to be an elder. That was the custom. This girl just had to obey her, work for her. Let her rest her tired bones after years of hard labor. But she refused. Fareeda was thirteen when she married, younger than this girl. And she'd worked and obeyed her mother-in-law. She'd taken care of her mother-in-law, her husband, her children, her own husband, without quarrel, without raising her head or complaining. She knew her time would come. And after ten years, it did—she bore a son. A glorious, beautiful son. Her own boy, her spitting image. He'd be hers, better than his weak, lazy father could ever be. And she waited for him to find a bride, for her time to come. But he didn't. And by then it was fine by her. Sometimes it was better not to have a daughter-in-law.

"You can't always trust brides," she finally hissed. "They lie and pretend they're something they're not. Like that one."

She spat on the floor in front of Yasmina.

"I told him she was a mistake. Filled with deceit and lies. But he said, because he's such a good son, *Mama, she'll take care of you when I'm gone. She'll feed you, clean the house, cook for you. Like you did with Ummi. You'll get to rest, Mama.* Such a good son. If he could, he would be here with me, taking care of me, and no stranger would walk into my house, and threaten me, and take what's mine. But he's in Belgika. He works so hard. Soon he'll come for me, you'll see. That girl you're holding, she's filth. She's a bad worker, she doesn't submit to the will of God, and her lust is overpowering. I smell it everywhere. Her dirt."

"All right, that's enough," Nayla said pushing her out of the way.

As they left Fareeda Boujloud's apartment and went down the stairs, Nayla held Yasmina tightly, lest the young girl's body snap under the weight of her anger and confusion, lest she herself surrender to her own rage. She tried to breathe her warmth into her, the warmth of an older, vibrant, resistant body.

Once they made it to the ground floor, they stopped. Nayla held Yasmina close and told her the words she told the women who came into her center, words she told herself, every day.

"Yasmina, we can't let fear and anger weigh us down. Just remember, we walk in the steps of others who came before us. People who were brave and stood up for women and children in this country, who sacrificed for us. Every step we take weaves us into the world. And the ones who came before us are always there, right beside us. Hold your head high, don't let anyone see you almost broke. Let them see you survived."

Yasmina looked at Nayla. She inhaled her beauty and fierce strength. Then she closed her eyes.

"Let's get this child something warm to eat," said Jamal, "and some rest, before we go anywhere."

They pushed open the building door. It was dark and cold out, but the moon was full and bright.

Yasmina wound the leather jacket tightly around her thin body, and Nayla's strong arm covered her shoulders.

# 12
## Cricket Café

The streets were dark except for the light of the moon and a few scattered street lights. They glimmered faintly here and there, strange fireflies in the still air. Far down the street, a single light flickered beneath a café awning.

Jamal led the way.

He knocked on the wood and glass door of Cricket Café and waited. The lights inside were on. Before long, the door was opened, and in front of them stood a short, thin man. He had a thin nose, thin mouth, thin cheeks, and deep blue eyes. The blonde hair still left on his head was interspersed with gray. On closer look, his thinness was all tight, sinewy muscle. He wore blue jeans, a black t-shirt, and worn-out, yellow leather *belgha,* traditional Moroccan footwear. He didn't seem surprised to see the ill-suited group that stood at his doorstep.

"Hello, Jo," said Jamal.

"Come on in," Jo answered gruffly.

"Silent type," Nayla whispered to Jamal.

Jamal smiled at her.

They followed the man through the dimly lit café to a

booth near the kitchen. After one look at his late-night clients, he nodded toward Yasmina.

"This kid needs to eat."

"Right," said Jamal.

Jo turned and disappeared into his kitchen.

"Jo?" asked Nadine.

"French, but I think he's forgotten that," Jamal smiled. "His family ran this café for ages. Then his parents died, his wife left him, and his kids went back to France. But he stayed."

"How come you know him?" asked Yasmina,

"We kind of worked together, a long time ago. I helped him out with some problems, and he's not the type to forget," said Jamal.

"What problems?" asked Yasmina.

"What are you, a detective?" Jamal said, trying to look stern. Then softening, he explained.

"When Jo's parents died, he was still young, not much more than a kid. Some bad people tried to take away the café from him. I used to come here a lot. I liked the place, I liked his parents. So I helped him keep it."

"How?" Yasmina asked again.

Jamal hesitated, then decided to tell.

"Before I was a journalist, in another lifetime, I knew some…people."

He leaned forward for effect.

"They bullied the bullies. And that was that."

"Cool!" said Yasmina.

Jamal burst out laughing.

"Yes, it was cool," he admitted.

Jo returned carrying a heavy tray. Holding it with one hand, he set on the table, eggs with *khlii*, Moroccan meat cured in ghee, sweet mint tea, Caobel (the mythical chocolate powder that warms a Moroccan childhood) in hot milk, toasted baguettes cut in half, butter, honey, and black olives.

"Eat," said Jo as he pushed plates toward Yasmina.

The trio drank their mint tea, and Jamal couldn't help but smile at Yasmina's appetite.

---

Yasmina put down her hot cocoa and leaned back.

"Let me tell you a little about us," Nayla said to her. "I work at a center for women whose children don't have a father to help raise them. Jamal is a journalist, and Nadine, she was Ghalia's employer. We want to find your sister and her child. We want to help her. And we want you to help us find her. Can you do that?"

Fear returned to Yasmina's eyes.

"You're not to blame for what happened, Yasmina. But if you know anything, tell us."

Yasmina turned to Nadine.

"You are Mrs. Mesari?"

"I am."

"And you want to help my sister?"

"I do."

"Mrs. Mesari, do you know what your husband did to her?"

"It seems to me that what happened was a mutual thing," she said as gently as she could.

"Mrs. Mesari, is that what you really think? That my sister wanted all this?"

The quiet around Nadine deepened as she thought

carefully about her next words. Words could be like wildfire, burning everything in their way, or they could be a lush, dark forest in whose lies one could get lost.

"I don't know what your sister wanted, Yasmina. What matters now is that we find Ghalia and her child. And I'm here to help."

"You don't believe she was a victim," said Yasmina.

Nadine was silent, unable to hurt, incapable of lying. The rot inside the lush forest was enveloping Nadine.

Nayla's voice dragged her out of the poisonous enchantment.

"Nadine," she said, roughing up her spiky hair with her hand. "This was about an employer forcing himself on his employee. Ghalia had other dreams than being with an older, married man. It's frightening to resist power. It corrupts everything."

"Why didn't she leave then? Why didn't she say something?" asked Nadine.

"Shame, fear, need."

"He threatened her," Yasmina interrupted. "He threatened to tell our family everything if she ever left your household. He wanted her there the whole time. Until…"

"…he found out she was with child," said Nayla.

Yamina nodded.

"No," said Nadine softly. "That can't be."

But the sickly rot's hold on her had weakened, and the lush forest was receding.

"He's a man, with his needs, but he's not cruel. He couldn't be that cruel," she hesitated, "unless…he was in love."

Jamal put down his coffee, now cold and barely touched, on the tabletop.

"Nadine, that isn't love. That could never be love."

"It could be what he believes is love," said Nayla.

"He wouldn't treat a woman like that, unless he was some kind of sociopath, or in love," said Nadine.

She breathed.

"Yasmina, where's your sister? Please."

The strength Yasmina had shown when they freed her seemed to be leaving her. She looked weak and distraught. Her fingers kept moving in a disconnected manner, back and forth, as though in a wordless prayer or in search of a lost path.

Nayla put her hand on hers.

"It's all right now. It's over. You don't need to be scared anymore."

Yasmina nodded, but hesitated. They waited. Then she spoke softly and quickly.

"My sister was the only person who was ever kind to me. My father, he's not the man he used to be. He only worries about pleasing my mother. And my mother, you met her, she only cares about appearances. *What will the neighbors think?* she always says, even though she despises them and speaks badly of them.

"So Ghalia came home with this little one in her arms, a beautiful little thing. The way she looked at him... But my parents they wanted them gone. I'm not sure my father really wanted them gone, but he did whatever my mother said. They told her to go, find a place. *You can't stay here,* they said.

"Ghalia had friends at school, these girls. They helped her in the beginning—food, a little money, stuff for the baby. They told her about your center for women like her. You're a legend, you know."

Yasmina glanced at Nayla who smiled sadly back at her, for it was from her center, after all, that Ghalia and the baby had been taken.

"So Ghalia went with the baby to your center. She put her life on hold, all her dreams, school, a job. She's so smart. Everyone wanted her to get rid of her baby. She could have gotten rid of him, but she didn't. She said he was here now. If she could be sure he'd be happier somewhere else, with other people who could really take care of him, she would let him go. But she didn't know anyone. She was the only one he had. So what choice did she have?"

Yasmina stopped and took a breath.

"When you told her about a journalist who could write down her story, who could fight for women like her and children like Noor," she said glancing at Nayla, then at Jamal, "she wasn't sure at first. But she wanted to help, to do what's right. She said yes. And that was the beginning of her problems. A rich man came to our house looking for her and the child. A man who threatened us. He knew people in high places. Dangerous people. But I didn't tell him where they were. I swear."

"You did the right thing," said Nayla.

"But nothing gets past my mother. She knew that I knew. And she decided to punish me, to wash herself of us. She married me off to that old, disgusting man. Then he went right back to Belgium and left me with that old witch. I was her maid, her slave. I could barely wash and had very little to eat. At night, she'd lock me up in that room."

Yasmina stopped.

"Then what happened?" asked Nadine.

"*He* found out where I was. My parents told him. He figured I'd know where Ghalia was," she paused, desperation in her eyes.

"So that's how he found her," said Jamal.

Yasmina lowered her head, tears fell down her cheeks.

"They came a couple of days ago to my mother-in-law's house. Two scary men and the rich one, his glasses hiding his face. He seemed scared of the other guys, too. But I knew who he was. They told my mother-in-law about Ghalia. She told them my parents tricked her. She said that *I* tricked her son into marrying me. They threatened me. They hurt me and *she* let them. But I didn't tell them anything, I swear."

"Even if you did," said Jamal, "you're not to blame."

"They looked in my phone and saw the messages. That's how they found her. This morning, one of the men made me go with him to your center, so that my sister could see me and be scared for me. They took her and the baby to this place, this terrible place and they brought me back. Fareeda Boujloud, my mother-in-law, locked me up in that room. Then you came."

Yasmina stopped and covered her face.

"How tough you are," said Nayla. "But you need to understand, it's not your fault."

Then it dawned on Nadine.

"Yasmina, did you send the newspaper article to my house?" she asked.

"Yes, I did. I don't know why. I just wanted you to know. Maybe to hurt like we were hurt. But mostly, to help us. To help the baby. He's yours, a little."

"Yasmina, I can't take the baby."

"But he'd be so much better off with you, if you found it in your heart to take him. After all, you're married to his father."

Then finally she told them.

"I heard them talk about a place, where they bring young girls and Blacks and poor people from other countries. And about the justice they serve there. It's called *L'Enfumoir.*"

"That place of nightmares," said Jamal, his voice rough. "People talk about it like it's some kind of hideout for hate in the city. I looked for it when I was a young journalist. I thought I'd find it, but never did. I'm not sure it's real," he shrugged.

Nayla nodded.

"A place many believe in, but few have seen, or survived to talk about. Women who come to our center say it's a court for the impure. I also heard it's a slave market like the ones that existed in the south of Morocco, where Blacks and women were sold. If Ghalia and Noor are there, they're in serious danger."

Yasmina interrupted them.

"It's real," she said. "And I know where it is."

They looked at her in surprise.

"I heard them mention it. But it's not a natural place. It's a terrible place, and you can get trapped there forever."

"Where is it, Yasmina?" asked Jamal.

"Oulad Taieb Street, in that old slum by the sea, on the other side of the city," she said.

Then, her eyelids suddenly heavy, Yasmina rested her head down on the table.

Sensing the toll of the past few weeks on their young friend, they watched her settle in to sleep.

———✦———

*Jo returned to clear the table.*

"Another kid lucky enough to bump into you, I see," he said as he picked up the empty plates. "Close the door behind you when you leave. This one's on me but don't get used to it," he called out quietly, already halfway in the kitchen.

The café turned still.

Nadine, Jamal and Nayla sat in silence, careful not to wake Yasmina up. Soon, Jamal's and Nayla's eyes closed, too.

Nadine listened to their breathing as it slowed and eased, suspending time itself. Strange, but this was the safest Nadine had felt in a long time.

Soon, her eyes closed, as well.

Time, that stretched and contracted at whim, reached out into the night toward the break of dawn.

# 13
# Village in the City

Nadine, Jamal, Nayla, and Yasmina got into the car. Nadine asked Nayla to drive and sat in the back, with Yasmina. Jamal sat in the front and entered the street name that Yasmina had given him on Waze—Oulad Taieb Street.

"Go," he told Nayla.

Yasmina shifted closer to Nadine and put her head on her shoulder. How tired she must be, thought Nadine and she wrapped an arm around her. She then took out her phone and dialed home. Jeanne answered. Her voice sounded both familiar and worlds away. Jeanne, the woman she had called *Zahra* all this time in her service.

Nadine had left her house on Saint Barthelemy Street less than twenty-four hours ago.

A day that could have been like any other had turned into a tale told by an accordion, one that compressed and expanded into other tales as she searched the city's maze of neighborhoods moved by a hope that a wrong could be made right.

She had a lightning quick thought: of this housekeeper's passport in her safe and the name on that passport that she had chosen to ignore. A name locked up because of her, just as the passport was. And in saying her name to her for the first time, she knew she needed to return her passport to her, and perhaps one day be forgiven this offense she had committed and had brushed aside as the mere legalistic constraints of hiring foreign workers.

"*Jeanne,*" said Nadine, a sigh of relief radiating through the word despite all her confusion and dread. "How are things at home? How's Al?"

Jeanne breathed softly as her body and mind inhaled the sounds of the simple syllables of her own name. And her contained anger rose and fell.

"She's well. She's waiting for you."

She hesitated for a moment.

"But her father went looking for you. He left early this morning. I think he knows where you are."

"How would he know?"

Jeanne paused again, then decided to trust her.

"Some men came to see him early this morning. I heard them talking. They said they had the woman and the child. But that a… well-dressed woman was looking for them, and she was with a journalist and a doctor."

"Where did they go?"

Jeanne's voice deepened.

"A very bad place. A place no one should go to. It's a name I've stumbled on before.

I heard your husband mention it on the phone. He seemed worried that something went wrong, that you may be in danger."

"What is this place?"

"*L'Enfumoir.*"

*L'Enfumoir—the bee smoker, a place that smoked people out.*

*Or trapped them in. It's the right place then,* Nadine thought to herself.

"There's something else."

"About Al?"

"Yes. She spoke, again. She said many things. To her father. I couldn't hear what she said, but I could see her."

"How did she seem?"

"The words tumbled out of her mouth like water from a spring. I couldn't hear her, but her face was bright, and the way she moved her hands and body was beautiful to see…alive, full of life. After listening to her, her father buried his face in his hands and I believe he cried, though men like him never cry."

"Do you know what she said to him?"

"I don't, but he listened carefully. Then he tried to take her hand, but she wouldn't let him. He's never been patient. I'm sorry, I shouldn't talk this way."

"Go on, Jeanne."

"Then, she raised her voice. And I think she said she saw things. That she knew what he'd done."

"What else did she say?"

"After that, I couldn't hear her anymore."

"Thank you, Jeanne," Nadine said and hung up.

Yasmina's head was heavy on her shoulder. She stared out the window as the car flew across the neighborhoods, and people took off their coats in the strange heat of a February morning.

"Al poured out her heart today," Nadine said, more to herself than to her companions. "And it's with her father she chooses to do so…"

"Daughters can be cruel to their mothers," said Nayla. "Be patient, have faith. You don't know what she knows about him or what she said to him. Wait and see."

Jamal stared at the map. The location of *L'Enfumoir* on the city map was one with which he was familiar. He leaned back on his seat.

"I know this place. It has to be the same place, even though it had no name then."

"How do you know about it?" asked Nayla.

"I tried investigating it, when I was starting up."

"Did you write anything?"

"I did. But the report was incomplete and not one of my best."

"Tell us. What are we getting into?" asked Nayla.

"It's where the French committed one of their worst crimes against this country."

Jamal collected his thoughts.

"The place we're headed to is on tribal homelands. The Oulad Taieb belonged to the Chaouia Confederation, Arab-Berber tribes. It was 1907. The Chaouia tribes rose up against the French invasion. In retaliation, the French massacred three thousand Chaoui in two days. They bombed them from the sea and attacked them by land. When the French troops moved in, they used their VB rifle grenades with discharger. Naval bombardment, then ground attacks—vengeance and terror more than warfare. The Ouled Taieb were among those whose people were decimated and whose land and villages were destroyed and taken over by the French."

"What about now, Jamal?" asked Nadine "What's happened to this land since then?"

"Any trace that this land belonged to a great tribal confederation, or that a colonial power waged a brutal war of pacification against it, was erased," said Jamal. "Now more than ever, the city's new, luxury coastal development plan is wiping the slate clean. Only one piece of ancestral land—what was its center—is left. Mostly empty, a no-man's land except for a poor, ignored population of slum-dwellers who, if they had any connection to the Oulad Taieb, they keep it to themselves. All that's left is one street name—Oulad Taieb Street."

Jamal examined the map carefully.

"*L'Enfumoir* could actually be the bull's eye of the French attack, the center of the Oulad Taieb massacre. A place of smoke and ashes that scattered a people like bees driven from their hive."

Nadine shivered.

"How big is the territory that's left? How long is the street we are going to?"

Jamal traced the street and the neighborhood on the map.

"Not as small as I thought," he said. "Why?"

"I don't know," she muttered, pondering the stolen lands in the city.

⁕

They had reached a fork in the road. To the right, the blue of the ocean brought out the brand new boardwalk and its vibrant colors of joggers, people walking their dogs, and young families taking a stroll. Perpendicular to the boardwalk, lining the sidewalk facing the sea, another world: street vendors, all women, all in white, selling snails in a spicy black broth, a beloved brew of locals.

To the left, the once gently rolling green hills that had been part of the confederation homeland, were dotted by residences and apartment complexes, some at least twenty years old, and others still under construction. *"Here we don't build houses, we build homes,"* were the words written on the sign hanging from the fence surrounding a behemoth building site.

Nadine took note of the slogan, a familiar one, and the buildings. *He has property here,* she thought.

They turned left toward the brand-new complexes, already broken down and graying with pollution dust, their promises for a better tomorrow unkept. Pressed between the luxury developments were low-built, wood, corrugated iron, and white stone dwellings resembling any Casablanca *bidonville.*

From up close, these structures seemed fragile and serpentine, about to be eaten up by redevelopment. But as they drove up the hills, the dwellings could be seen for what they really were: a village within a city. Entering from any point, one could quickly get lost in its web of dirt paths.

---

When they reached Oulad Taieb Street, they stopped and got out. It turned out to be a nondescript side road, bordered on one side by empty lots filled with cattle, chicken, and children's toys; and on the other by openings, like punctures, in the corrugated and stone walls of the slum.

"This is just another street. There's nothing here," said Yasmina.

"We have to go in," answered Nayla.

"Not even the police go in here," said Jamal. "The only time anyone does is to bulldoze a few rows of houses to make way for developments."

Yasmina trembled.

Jamal turned to her.

"Stay here. No need for you to come. Stay in the car," he said gently.

He opened the car door for her and she lay down on the back seat.

Then, one by one, Nadine, Nayla and Jamal went in through an opening between the walls.

———————

After a short distance on the dirt road, they encountered a man sitting on a plastic stool in front of a corrugated iron door, painted green, most likely the door to his house.

He was whittling away at a wooden figure as wood shavings fell, one by one, around his feet. The old man wore worn corduroy pants, a gray shirt, and a whitish-brown, imitation Panama hat. His brown face was thin and deeply lined, and his white beard and gray hair made his age difficult to guess. He had the look of a Casablanca factory worker from the eighties, a tough, leathery man whose eyes betrayed his abandonment. The look-alike Panama hat and the corduroy pants were a legacy from the French era, a status symbol for those workers who had become foremen or assembly line supervisors—now the sign of a betrayed working-class culture warped into a disappointed assimilation. He barely raised his eyes from his work.

"Friends," he said, as he whittled at the piece with his pen knife. "What are you looking for in the cemetery of the Ouled Taieb?"

His Arabic was tense and hard; an Arabic wrought out in Casablanca factories, in its quenched struggles and lost battlegrounds.

Nayla stepped forward.

"Hello, sir. We don't usually come into other people's territory without notice," she said.

Jamal glanced at her, amused. This was a blatant lie, since her life as a combatant for women's and children's rights was a series of unannounced, unwanted entries into other people's territory and business. The old man replied, switching from Arabic to a near perfect-French.

"*Amis ou ennemis?*" he asked, "friend or foe?"

"*Amis de ceux qui recherchent la justice,*" answered Jamal, mirroring his words, "friends to those who seek justice."

The old man nodded, a thin smile on his lips, and Nayla continued:

"We're looking for a young woman and her child. We believe she's here."

"Many women, many children are here," he replied. "Foreigners who come to rest, trying to escape their past. What's special about these two?" This time his sharp eyes turned to Nadine before looking back down.

"She's been taken to a place called *L'Enfumoir*. We believe it's here. And we believe she's in danger."

He passed his rough, brown hand through his beard.

"You've been lied to. There's no such place here, or anywhere."

"We've been told it's somewhere around here. We mean no trouble. But we need to find this woman and her child and get them somewhere safe, before it's too late."

He shook his head repeatedly.

"I tell you, there's no such place here. We're just an old slum living our last days."

They looked at him, their disappointment palpable. After a calculated pause, the old man knelt forward.

"Once we were an honored people. Who cares about that now?"

"Who hasn't heard of the great tribes of the Chaouia and their heroic battle against the invaders?" said Jamal.

The old man eased his back into the wall of his house, and when he next spoke, his voice was warm and deep.

"Our children see the bulldozers and the growing holes at their doorsteps. It's only a matter of time before what's left is taken from us. After the great war of the Chaouia, they corrupted what was left of our chiefs, bought them off with land and gold, and left us here. Almost all our land has been taken away. It's up for grabs. We can remind our youth that these lands are our lands. But what does that matter when the city has other plans for us all?"

The old man worked his knife finely on the piece of wood, patiently transforming it into a kneeling figure. He put it down and picked up another piece of wood. As he inspected it in his palm, preparing to whittle at it, a barefoot little girl with golden skin, light brown eyes, curly blonde hair, and pink sweatpants and sweatshirt, came running out of the house from behind him and jumped into his lap.

He laughed, a kind, youthful laugh, and stroked her hair.

"My granddaughter. What's left of my blood-line," he told them. "The mother died in the beginning of summer, and the father went looking for work in the Moroccan south, or so he said before the road ate him up. Sometimes the father calls his daughter and cries. But what good do the tears of a grown man do for a little girl?"

Her name was Kenza, *treasure* in Arabic.

The old man held her close in the crook of his arm as he continued to whittle.

"Tell them, Grandpa, tell them. That little baby was so cute. I don't want him to get hurt."

He looked at her, trying to be stern, but then he weakened and sighed, kissing the hair that mingled in his beard.

"I used to work in a factory. We made shirts for Europe. But then the Chinese opened their factories. You can't compete with them. No one could tell the difference between their shirts and ours. My factory closed and I lost my job. So now I do this. I make wooden figureheads and talismans and sell them on the streets or to vendors in the Habbous, in the old town. Until no one will want to buy my work anymore or until my eyes fail me or my fingers become knots. And all I'll have left are my stories, and this child. But to each time its woes."

Jamal glanced at the women who were carefully listening to their exchange, gauging their every word.

"We were warriors and poets once. The old ones go and the new ones come. But traces remain. Of light, those who keep our ways alive, our knowledge. And of darkness, those who only want to avenge the past and take it out on others weaker than themselves," he went on.

The old man continued to whittle at the piece. They all held their breath.

"There's a place down the dirt road. It's a house like this one, made of corrugated iron, stone and wood. But with a red door, as old as mine." He leaned back, "The old folk used to say that was where the bombs fell, where the soldiers did their dirtiest work. Death was in their bones and there was no stopping them. The people had been smoked out of their beds and killed.

For days, the village was filled with smoke, ash and the smell of burning bodies," he said. He put down the piece, a child, and picked up a third, knotted piece of wood.

"Some nights, we can still smell burning flesh and hear the screams of the disappeared. There was no place to hide then, and there's no place to hide now. So how could *L'Enfumoir* be here?"

But he pronounced it *"L'Enfermoir"*—the place where people are locked in. Or was it *"L'Enfernoir,"* the black inferno?

The old man had just whittled a flower. He bore a hole in one of its petals, close to its center, and passed a string through it. He then put it around the little girl's neck as she clapped her hands in glee. He picked up another piece of wood.

Slowly, finally, they understood.

"And where is the house with the red door?" Nadine asked.

He pointed toward his left with the pen knife.

"Go down this road, straight. Count seven side streets, to your left, to your right. At the seventh side street, go right. The dirt road gets darker, redder, softer on the feet. Keep going down that road. But know that it's a no-man's land. From there, you're on your own. No one can help you. You will think it's just another slum, but you'll see they're not corrugated iron homes. They're what's left of our village. The houses have all been emptied of their people. Only ghosts still roam. Sometimes you can hear them at night. Wails and iron hooves. Stone and steel made grief. The last sighs of my people's great forgotten war and of our disappearance. To go there, deep into our lands, is to seek what you can't find—mercy for the enemy, compassion for the fallen foe."

They thanked him for his help. He shook his head.

Again, almost as a protection, he kissed the little girl's head.

Then he got up, indicating that their time with him was over.

# 14

# Red Door

They set out on foot to find the house with the red door. As they walked, they counted off the seven streets, which were lined sparsely with trees, and without sidewalks. They passed children playing in the streets, women doing their laundry in big water buckets and chatting easily among themselves, men smoking and playing cards. No one bothered them, or even really looked at them. It was almost as though they knew they were coming and what they were looking for. A few women averted their eyes, held their children near, and waited for them to pass.

But the farther they walked, the quieter the streets became. People shut their doors and the only sound that remained was that of leaves rustling in the wind.

When they reached the seventh street, they turned right onto a muddy dirt road. The houses seemed deserted, their stone and iron sheeted walls unkempt and broken down. As they walked, they noticed a faint buzzing coming from what sounded like an electric appliance or a mechanical toy. Nadine paused to listen and then started walking toward the noise.

"We're not supposed to roam off. It may not be safe," Jamal cautioned her.

But Nadine just kept going. They watched her for a moment but then followed her toward the dull metallic noise.

The sound led them to one of the abandoned houses on a side street. Peering into the house through a glassless window, they could see three rows of what looked like textile machinery. Beneath each machine, steel rings were anchored to the ground with chains attached to them. Suspended above the rows of machines, as if suspended in thin air, was a larger machine, its wheels, spikes, and turbines whirring for an unknown purpose.

"A sweatshop," said Nadine. "The ghosts the old man mentioned hearing at night, maybe they're the men and women who work here."

"How many sweatshops are hidden here?" asked Nayla. They walked to the next house, and the next. In house after house, they found the same setup of textile machinery. "Sweatshops. And right in the heart of the city, on the most valuable coastal land. How do they get away with this?"

"They get away with this until something more valuable comes along, or someone more powerful sets his sights on this place," said Jamal. "Let's get going."

And they followed his thick figure back to their path.

The dirt road opened onto the square the old man had mentioned. It was lined with dilapidated houses and vacant lots filled with rubble. And straight ahead of them, at the center of the square and set at an odd angle stood the house with the red door.

There was no sign of life or movement.

As they approached the house, holes in the walls—oval, regular, man-made—became visible. The ruins had similar holes. This must be the old heart of the Ouled Taieb village, bombed by the French in the 1907 uprising of the Chaouia Confederation.

There was shrapnel, still, in some of these holes.

"So this is *L'Enfumoir,*" said Nadine.

Reaching the house, they pushed open the red door.

———————

Inside the house with the red door was a single, square, medium-sized room. It was totally empty and deserted. It was the house's only room, where a family once cooked, ate, and slept side by side.

"Where are the stairs?" asked Nayla. "Was the old man lying to us?"

They wandered around the room. Nothing.

Nadine stopped in the center of the room and just stood there, baffled. But then she felt something cold and smooth under her feet. She brushed aside the dirt, and there appeared to be a smooth stone.

"Wait. There's something here," she said.

Nayla and Jamal joined her, and, kneeling around it, they swept the stone clean with their hands. It was black and cut into a rectangle.

Nayla pushed hard against it, and the stone slid downward. Plainly visible was a staircase descending into the darkness below.

# 15

## L'Enfumoir

They turned on their phone lights and followed one another—
Nayla first, then Nadine, then Jamal—down the wide, stone
stairs into the dark. The stairway was long and windy, and
they had to step carefully to keep their footing on the stone.

As they descended, the darkness deepened and the air
became colder and more humid. Then their feet touched soft
ground, like freshly turned earth, or sand. It felt as though
they were entering a grotto beneath the sea.

The walls and ceiling were a brown rock that curved
down into the earth. They found themselves in a cave that
continued on into many chambers. They raised their phones
to better see what was around them and continued walking,
one behind the other.

"There are footsteps here," said Nadine as she pointed her
phone in front of her.

Nayla and Jamal followed Nadine through the cavern. In
the distance, they could hear the sound of waves crashing
against the shore, as if they were inside a seashell.

Other sounds began to cover the sound of the crashing
waves.

They stopped and listened.

Voices, angry, not far off, could be heard reverberating off the walls.

They walked as quickly and as silently as possible, following the voices, howls in the night, rough rhythms in the still air.

---

The cavern widened into a large chamber, and it took a few moments for their eyes to adjust to the surroundings. Ancient bones were stacked against the walls. A catacomb.

The voices were all around them now, men's voices, brutal and indecipherable. Behind the voices, was another sound, lower, more muffled—*thump, thump*—like wood on sand, or stone on cloth. Then higher, softer sounds. The different sounds rose and receded, billowed and lowered.

They quickened their pace.

They heard another muffled sound, like footsteps on wet clay, and the voices began to recede away into the distance, as if through another tunnel.

Nadine stopped and turned to look at her companions. They too had stopped and were listening intently.

The sounds had ceased.

Their light their only remaining compass in the darkness, they walked down the path.

---

Soon after, they entered another chamber. It was above a circular alcove that appeared to be a natural arena. The ground was wet, the chamber completely still. They looked down into the arena, trying to see into the darkness. Nothing.

Then, slowly, as their eyes adjusted, in the center of the

ash-colored arena they saw a huddled shape—a woman's rounded back and arms. Her body lay still, her clothes torn and darkened and reddened. She was curled up protectively around another, smaller shape—a child.

Stones and glass littered the ground around them.

Whatever hopes and persistence had brought them this far were extinguished, like a small fire by hailstone.

They ran down the path, their feet hitting the uneven ground, into the arena.

They knelt next to Ghalia.

Her large, almond eyes were closed, and her skin was cold. And though her perfect mouth, heavy, auburn hair, and golden-brown skin still shone with the hints of the intense joy and courage that had been hers not so long ago, they knew she was gone.

But, somehow, the baby was still breathing.

Nayla smoothed Ghalia's hair, and Jamal lowered his head into his hands, as Nadine gathered Noor in her arms.

<hr />

After a while, Nayla stood up, feeling as old as time itself. Jamal picked Ghalia up. And they set off to retrace their footsteps. There was a long way to go to reach the car.

Nadine followed them, holding Noor carefully against her. His body was cold. But if she held him close to her chest, he would feel her warmth. The child closed his eyes and buried his nose against her neck.

A thought, lightning quick and unutterable, crossed her mind. Would it not have been simpler if the little boy, too, had been taken by death, and not just Ghalia. How soft and kind death would be. The child's suffering would cease, and his uncertain future would be erased from the stars.

But then the child opened his eyes, deep and dark, and he reminded her of another child, long gone. He looked like him. Nadine's heart beat faster, and she felt something she hadn't felt in many years—alive.

—◈—

They walked up the path that led out from the cave and back into the house with the red door. When they went out into the graying sunlight, the world seemed a strange and unexpected place.

The old factory worker carving wooden pieces was gone, his third and final wooden piece, in the shape of a key, lay on the ground. The playful little girl was gone, too. In fact, the entire slum village appeared deserted, as though its inhabitants had suddenly fled, or gone into hiding.

Nayla and Jamal walked side by side, carrying Ghalia between them. Nadine followed behind them.

She could feel Noor's heartbeat and his intense desire for life, and it echoed her own.

He took in the clean, crisp air. How many threads had been woven together, destinies intertwined, for Noor to see the light of day?

# 16

# Cave of Whispers

The cave filled with a long, deep silence, almost like a hushed wail, or the endless depth of a starless night. An ashen, restless sigh created by what it had witnessed for centuries, and on this very day. And then the silence lifted to reveal the whispers beneath.

A young woman and her child were stoned on this day by a gang of young men, some of whom were known to her. The young men were paid to find her and give her up to the police, along with her child born out of wedlock, and as demanded by the powerful man who had once claimed to love her. But instead of turning her in, their hatred of her—of her transgressions and weaknesses, but also of her intelligence and dreams—had turned their hunt into a vendetta.

But the child survived and was retrieved from the darkness; its future uncertain, but alive and free.

———※———

This could have been a good place, a place of faith and shelter for outcasts and the defenseless. For *L'Enfumoir* was born from the 1907 Arab and Berber peoples uprising against invasion and occupation, and their massacre by heavily armed French forces. It could have become Casablanca's breathing soul.

Instead, it had become colonized as a place of power by those who remembered only the trauma, not the bravery and the life before it. And like all places of power, this one was woven around tales of crimes committed, pain inflicted, victories stolen. Other tales became intertwined in this deep, dark story, and it became the repository of the city's unwanted, unpeeled histories, its unwilling receptacle: a breeding ground for slave markets, ancient and perhaps new, street justice, extrajudicial tribunals, religious vendettas and rough fantasies.

But the child had survived, and the cave once more was witness to bravery and kindness, after more than a century of darkness. Perhaps now, history would go around another bend in the road and the cave's whispers heard for what they always were: its vigil, its soft, endless song against voiceless-ness and brutality—its story of remembrance.

# Part IV

# 17
# Of Slaves and Daughters

*Time, the accordion*

Over the cherry wood dressing table, in the far corner of Nadine's room in the house on Saint Barthelemy Street, hung the antique mirror that had belonged to her mother, and to her grandmother before her.

The mirror's rectangular shape, with sides dipping low, resembled an accordion. With silver frame and coated with a toxic mercury that may have sickened or killed its maker, the glass was spidered and cloudy in places. Nadine had had it cleaned, though not too much. It wasn't a practical mirror, for it reflected its owner in a haze, just as she herself was now a pale reflection of her earlier, simpler self.

She'd sit in front of it, brushing her hair, putting on her lipstick, or just reading, and think of the women—her grandmother, then her mother—who had sat in front of it before her. They too had brushed their hair, applied their makeup, and gazed into its depths. She didn't know what they longed for, but she knew they longed. That seemed to her to be the actual reason for the existence of mirrors: not to reflect, but to allow longing…and escape.

*"Mirror, mirror on the wall,"* she would whisper to it playfully when no one was around. *"Who is the saddest of them all?"*

Nadine enjoyed her twist on the popular fairy tale where the stepmother used the mirror to cradle her longing for her stepdaughter's youth and beauty. And the mirror of the fairy tale would answer, *"Not you, never you,"* each time deepening her longing, exacerbating her desire, plunging her, little by little, into madness. If her mirror were to answer, it would say, *"You, always you."* And her solitude would deepen.

*"Mirror, mirror on the wall, tell me of the quiet and monotony of passing days, of graying hair, of wrinkling skin, of dimming eyes."*

Nadine thought of these women before her, who sat in front of this mirror as their dreams faded and their hopes blemished. Sometimes, on desperate days, she thought of it as a cycle: we are trapped in the glass's recurrent reflection, its image of us. But on days when the sun shone gently, it seemed to her a place of power, and she found refuge there, in front of it, the only place in the house where she could be enveloped in softness and haze.

The day Nadine received the newspaper clipping about a single mother and her little boy, she had locked herself up in her room and looked into the mirror. It was her reference point when faced with difficult decisions. She stared into its depths looking for answers, or more precisely, saying goodbye to her old self. The day she uprooted her life, Nadine sat in front of the looking glass as her thoughts meandered back to her roots, to who she was told she was, and who she thought she was.

———

Nadine's maternal grandfather was Hassan Raiss, the son of the great Mohamed Raiss. They were a wealthy merchant family from Fes who had migrated to Casablanca and succeeded in adapting to the new marketplace that thrived there. Their fortune was in textiles and real estate.

Nadine's mother, Alia Raiss, had married Omar Alam, a French-trained engineer. Theirs was a quiet marriage, scandal-free and discreet. But friends and neighbors did comment on how thin and tired Alia often seemed, and how the husband kept to himself, played the 'oud, and read books by the window, a routine he'd interrupt only to disappear for days, until he left for good. As she lay in bed one final day, after losing the battle against her illness, Nadine's mother told her that strength was a woman's greatest apparel and that they had a treasure trove of it. For *her* mother—Nadine's grandmother—was Maryam Peña, and Nadine must have faith in that legacy, in her own hidden, quiet strength, and never despair.

Nadine was thirteen when her mother died. And when she went to live with her father and his new wife, she kept her mother's dying words clutched in her heart.

---

The Peñas were a Moroccan family of Jewish faith, exiled from Andalusia, who had in the twentieth century spread their roots across the world. Almost all of them left Morocco in the twentieth century, except for Nadine's grandmother Maryam, who had married Hassan Raiss.

At the time Maryam and Hassan fell in love, theirs was a forbidden love, for in the forties, Jews and Muslims who embraced, fell in love, and then chose to marry were considered traitors to their communities.

When their daughter Alia—Nadine's mother—was born, Maryam and Hassan's shared joy was great, even though

Maryam turned her attention to her little girl, and Hassan was no longer the sole object of her affections. Maryam and Hassan even survived the death of their second little girl, born just a year after their first, though Maryam's sadness, which she hid from him as best she could, was too great for her to ever fend off.

All this changed when Hassan Raiss's father, the great, towering Mohamed Raiss, died.

Hassan was the only male heir, and at his father's death, he inherited the bulk of his father's vast fortune. His sisters and mother, according to Muslim custom, only received half of his share.

Hassan changed. He was now a rich and powerful man, and simplicity was gone from his life. He began to act, and look, like his father: short beard, arrogant mien, low voice. He started wearing perfectly tailored suits on all days except Fridays, when he donned the traditional white *djellaba* and soft, yellow leather *belgha*. He rarely came home anymore, nor did he express affection toward, or even look at, Maryam or their little girl.

Maryam was quick to understand that Hassan's transformation was definitive, that he would soon break her heart, and perhaps even discard her and her little girl.

Maryam wrote to her father, Abraham Peña, who lived in Brooklyn, New York. She asked that he give her the house they had once lived in, before Morocco's independence from the French. The house was in Casablanca, in the Oasis neighborhood, whose streets bore the name of flying insects and beasts, flowers and trees. Also, it was close to the city's only Jewish Museum, once a synagogue, which Maryam believed to be magical when she was a little girl. She asked for this house on Butterfly Street, Abraham's last remaining

Moroccan possession, and the first house they had lived in as a family.

Abraham Peña was not an easy man to contend with, nor was he known to give freely. But he listened to the voice of the daughter he hadn't seen or spoken to in over five years. After a long silence, he answered.

"Yes."

Soon thereafter, a lawyer contacted Maryam with the deed to the house and documents to sign.

She waited for Rabbi Ygal Aflalo to accompany her to the Administration of Hebraic Affairs, as her father instructed her to do. She hadn't seen the rabbi since the day in their home when she told her father she would marry a Muslim man. The rabbi had barely aged, except that now in his beard the white intermingled with the silver and the black.

"What your father did for you to have this house, my child. What the community accepted to do, for you, our wayward child. But we cannot say no to Abraham Peña, for he has done a great deal for our people."

Maryam didn't answer, the destructive powers of belonging—to captivate, mislead, forget, even erase—being a poisonous relic of the past for her.

The rabbi took her to the Hebraic Affairs office, and after a lengthy wait, the house was hers, and hers to give to her only daughter, Alia. And then Maryam went to her husband and did something unheard of: she asked him for a divorce.

Before letting her go, along with the daughter he had no use for, Hassan reminded her that divorce was a man's prerogative.

In truth, he was relieved that she was the one to ask, he wouldn't have to look into her piercing black eyes and smell her jasmine scent, or admit that he had been too great a coward, too weak a man, to resist the glistening outer shell of wealth and status, and stay still in the quiet of her arms.

Maryam took Alia and moved into the decrepit, but welcoming, house on Butterfly Street, in the Oasis neighborhood.

There she remained with her daughter, refusing to leave Casablanca, even after most of Casablanca's Jewish community had left for Paris, Montreal, New York, or Tel Aviv.

On her deathbed, she bequeathed the house to her daughter Alia and told her to bequeath it to *her* daughter after her, as had been granted them by their community, one whose harsh rabbinic rules her father knew how to bend to his will for his only daughter.

Abraham refused to meet his granddaughter Alia, just as he had refused to ever see Maryam again, his daughter whom he had loved most of all in this world, more even than tradition itself.

But the house on Butterfly Street was never home only to Maryam and her daughter, Alia. Another woman and her child sought refuge there. And although their place there would always be one of subservience and discomfort, Nadine wouldn't see this until much later in her life, when she would try, perhaps too late, to remedy that original sin.

———— ❧ ————

When the French took control of Morocco in the beginning of the twentieth century, they declared slavery illegal, an evil and senseless practice. And yet, the urban hovels, houses, and palaces, the *ksars* and *kasbahs*—fortified villages, and citadels—continued the practice, ignoring the decree. The colonizer failed to understand that indentured peoples often have no place to go and would remain in the houses that had enslaved them, and that, even after the decree, slave and servant were barely a breath removed from one another. The new servants, captured in their youth, forever cut from their families and lands, had barely ever stepped outside their masters' domains, and most would never leave. For they feared the world beyond the walls.

This was the case for Yacout, whose real name lies buried in the desert sands between present-day Mali and Mauritania. She was kidnapped in a slave raid in which nearly all the children and young men and women of her village were captured, except for the chief's own children and grandchildren, for alliances between the rich and powerful crisscrossed the desert sands and transcended ethnic loyalties. She never saw her people—not her mother or father, sisters or brothers, whose names and face she couldn't recall—ever again.

She came to Fes speaking only Bambara and the Arabic she learned in her masters' house as a child, an Arabic infused with Bambara song and sound. As the years passed, she forgot her native language, remembering only its echoes.

But even its faint echoes were of some shelter to Yacout when, in the middle of the day, or of the night, or whenever suited his pleasure, the old, lecherous Mohamed Raiss would rape her, and tell her she was the most beautiful and sweet-tasting of all the budding flowers in his household. This master of the house who was Nadine's great-grandfather, and most probably Amber's grandfather.

Even though the household was filled with women who belonged to him, Mohamed Raiss had only one legitimate wife, Daouia Raiss—Maryam Peña's formidable mother-in-law. Despite the decree declaring slavery illegal, Daouia was unfazed and showed the world that, in all matters, she was in agreement with her husband; especially so in matters of servants who could be sold as slaves, or used in the kitchen or in the master's bedroom.

When her son, Hassan Raiss, married Maryam Peña, Daouia gave her new daughter-in-law a gift—a young woman and her daughter. The young woman was called Yasmine. She was the daughter of Yacout and most certainly of Daouia's husband, Mohamed Raiss. Yasmine's daughter was called Amber, still a child and of unknown father.

And although women like Yasmine were told by the French colonial administration that they were now free, it changed nothing in either Daouia's—or Yasmine's—understanding of their places in the world.

And so, the one named Amber, though born fifteen years after the decree, was and would remain enslaved and become a star forever imprisoned in a family's night sky.

———✦———

Nadine's grandmother Maryam was kind enough to Yasmine and Amber. But she wasn't sure what to do with them in her home—she who wanted to be alone with her husband, which was impossible in those days.

Her mother-in-law humorously admonished her.

"When your children are born, Yasmine will take care of them, and she will teach her daughter Amber to take care of them, and of their children after them. You'll see the need for them then."

"Amber's still nearly a child," tried Maryam, again.

"She's smart and strong, although her tongue is too sharp for her own good," Daouia chuckled, playfully hitting Amber on the side of the head.

Amber's eyes lit up with a dangerous light that she quickly hid.

But later, when Maryam and Hassan divorced, he kept—at his mother's insistence—Yasmine and her daughter, Amber, by now a young woman.

"They belong to this house, to you, not to that woman," his mother insisted.

So Daouia took back her son and her servants.

She then chose a new wife for him: Fatiha Benkash. A young, strong woman, she thought, one who would bear him sons and manage his household like a commander.

<hr>

Hassan Raiss's new wife, Fatiha Benkash, feared Yasmine and Amber.

After losing her first two children in the womb, Fatiha became convinced that she had been poisoned, bewitched. And the only one who possessed such power was Yasmine, who had been taught black magic by her mother Yacout.

The new wife wanted the master for herself, and Yasmine and her daughter were a threat to her.

"You must know your place and what's allowed, lest you lose it all," Fatiha warned Yasmine.

Yasmine knew that the new wife could throw her and her daughter to the curb without any qualms, for it wasn't to her that she owed her allegiance.

And Fatiha Benkash wasn't stupid. She saw the way her husband looked at Amber, still young but already a woman, how enthralled he was by her.

"Yasmine is Voodoo. Our children are dead because of her. One of your daughters by your Jewish wife is dead because of her. You never had a son because of her. And now, your financial misfortune is because of her," she told Hassan one dark night as they lay in bed, his body between her thighs.

"Send her and her daughter away."

What Fatiha did not know, and what her husband Hassan Raiss did not care to know, was that Yasmine was the daughter of Mohamed Raiss and his servant-slave Yacout. That Yasmine was thus related to Hassan himself. It wasn't a fact that he would ever wish to know, because he himself had been with Yasmine, and other women of the house—at his own mother's insistence, and before he'd ever laid eyes on Maryam and believed he was healed forever, free from his world's demands and tyranny.

Hassan realized that Yasmine, and her daughter Amber, had nowhere else to go. Even so, he sent them away, not only to please his young wife but because he too saw the hatred and strength that seethed beneath Amber's dark eyes and swift gait. But mostly, he sent them away because they reminded him of Maryam Peña and their first years of marriage. Years when they believed their love was stronger than family, than tradition, than religion, than caste—than place of man and woman or slave and master. He sent them away, in truth, because he, too, believed that they had cursed him.

───────

Yacout was a woman Nadine had heard stories about for nearly her entire life. She was a mythical, almost magical woman, but one known only as "Dada," "Nurse," "Slave"—both one and legion, woman and thing. Attached to a household, beloved by the masters' children, mother perhaps even to some of the masters' children, and utterly disposable.

Nadine had heard the vague rumor that circulated in her grandmother Maryam's home since she herself was a child: that Yasmine was related to Hassan, his half-sister on the Raiss side. Therefore, she was not only Nadine's nanny and servant, but also her great-aunt: skin tamarind brown and hair dark and thick, where Nadine's skin was cream-colored and her hair golden.

But Nadine firmly believed that those were *other* times, when the master of the house, and even his sons, could take whichever servant girl they pleased. There were even beliefs that the darker and the younger the servant, the more powerful was her magic and her ability to invigorate and make potent the aging patriarch or his prepubescent sons. It was all about exercising an ancestral power. But sometimes, love seeped in—a child's love, hurt and soft, a woman's love, mangled and burning, a man's love, perverted and unquenchable.

Those times, thought Nadine, were long gone. They were old stories, of which she only knew bits and pieces, for they were not easy or simple stories to tell.

But Amber remembered the wrongdoings, the cold, dark secrets. They were tales of the rights of men over women, of Arabs over Blacks, of patriarchs over children. They were tales too harsh for a pretty little girl like Nadine to ever understand. And they mustn't be spoken about, Amber would warn her, for those days could return, like the boogie man.

Instead, Amber would sing for her.

She would take Nadine into her heavy arms and rock her against her chest and sing to her until she closed her eyes, safe and warm against her.

Nadine always loved Amber's songs.

"Those are strange words in there. What do they mean?" she would ask.

Amber would nod and stroke Nadine's back with her large, rough hands and tell her that she didn't know either; that the songs' meanings were lost in the fog of the past. And Nadine would just say, "I love them."

The Gnawa, whose music, drumming and words curled through Amber's songs, brought listeners into trance. The musicians, in fact a Sufi confederation, say that they too don't know the meaning of most of their words, and songs. Stolen as children from their homelands, villages in the desert oases, or in open coastal waterways, they say they invented words, or rather that they recalled sounds and rhythms from their childhood as through a strainer, or a broken record.

But it was Amber's voice that Nadine loved most. She, like many people, didn't listen to words in a song. And that's for the best.

⋯⟐⋯

After having been forced out of Fatiha and Hassan Raiss's household—the only home they knew, Yasmine and Amber went to the only place they knew in the world beyond the walls: Maryam Peña's house on Butterfly Street.

They knew she understood exile. They had seen it in her eyes.

She took them in.

And she was kind to them.

Except for that one time, which Amber tried to bury deep inside her chest.

⋯⟐⋯

One day, a young man started coming to work in the small garden at the back of the house. He came twice, sometimes three times a week, and Amber would watch him from the house as he worked. He weeded and planted and watered. The garden bloomed under his touch. His name was Idriss.

A few months passed, and Amber told Idriss that she was with child. And the child was his.

The next day, he didn't come to work, nor the day after.

Amber never saw or heard from him again.

When Yasmine found out her daughter was pregnant, she dragged her into the kitchen and beat her black and blue with the rolling pin she used to knead the bread.

"You stupid, stupid girl!"

After a time, Yasmine could no longer hide her daughter's condition, and she told Maryam that Amber was with child. Nadine's grandmother advised her, at once gentle, cold, wise, and a little off, as was her way.

"We'll find a solution. But the baby can't stay here. You're lucky you and your daughter can stay after what she did. But I'm attached to you, and I don't put women out on the street."

A few months later, Amber gave birth—to a baby girl.

Yasmine and Maryam took the child away.

And after that, Amber became the dark, terrifying, and inscrutable woman she was known to be for the rest of her life, her laughter and the deep-brown warmth of her eyes, their honey sweetness, gone for good, or so it appeared.

Amber saw her daughter only once after that day. She went to Marrakesh, to the address given her by her mother, where she found the little girl, then eight years old and a scullery maid in the house of one of Maryam Peña's friends.

Many years later, Amber heard news of her daughter's death. She took a week off from her work in Kamal and Nadine's house, the only week she had ever taken off, and went to her daughter's funeral in Marrakesh.

There she paid the funeral expenses for the skinny little girl she had seen just once, the child of the one man she ever loved. Then she returned to Casablanca.

No one asked any questions, and it was better that way.

Only Jeanne, the Senegalese housekeeper working with them, asked, but Amber wouldn't say. She didn't trust Jeanne. Her skin black as coal, her eyes proud, and her speech poised. As though she thought she was better than Amber, as though the color of your skin—how dark, how golden, how light—was not everything in this country.

# 18
# Ghalia

During the hot summer months, whenever her friends asked Ghalia to come to the beach with them, or to go out for a shawarma and fries, she'd say she couldn't, she was working.

She explained to them that she needed the money to finish her studies. When they asked her more about this mystery nonstop job she had, she said, "I work with these people, a family." She wouldn't tell them what the job was. She wouldn't say, "I'm a maid, I clean up their messes and obey their orders." It was just she had a job, like any job.

The important thing was to communicate to them, and convince herself, that it wouldn't be permanent, that it wasn't part of who she was. She knew young women, like some of her friends, who abandoned their studies, or whose degrees were worthless and who ended up being full-time maids, with no end in sight. She would never let that happen to herself. It was just a summer job.

Then Covid happened and university stopped. The family she had worked for during the summer, the Mesaris, asked her if she would be willing to stay on until her school opened its doors again. Ghalia gladly accepted the offer. Of course she would, she'd have access to the Internet and free time to study. And it allowed her to escape her family and the apartment they shared.

Ghalia's people on her father's side came from the countryside. Her father had dreamed of being an engineer, but wasn't able to stay in school past age fourteen. He had to work to help his parents out. He went to the big city and learned to become a mechanic, in a garage in Ben M'sik. He deferred to her his dream of studying, of learning how things work on the inside, of becoming an engineer.

Ghalia's mother's people were from the city. Ben M'sik, born and raised over three generations. Tough, inside and out, and intolerant. They had forgotten their rural roots and looked down upon newcomers from the countryside. Just as they had looked down on Ghalia's father. And just as Ghalia's mother now looked down on him too, for his salary and ambition had barely changed over the years. She was the main bread earner and despised him for it. And he was completely under her power, except when he tried to comfort Ghalia and shield her from her mother's biting words, times that were few and far between.

Ghalia's mother looked at her the same way she looked at her father: with barely concealed contempt, rage even, despite all Ghalia's attempts to be good, to be ambitious, to work hard. Instead, she was "just like her father, dark skin, head full of dreams, unfit for the real world."

Her father would tell her, softly so that her mother didn't hear him, but with a twinkle of pride in his eyes, "You're the brightest, most beautiful person I know. And my little princess." And then Ghalia would stop wishing her skin was white, like her mother's or her sister's, or the pretty girls' skin at school and on TV. In fact, she tried not to think of the way she looked at all and was always surprised when others saw her as beautiful or told her she was, for she didn't think of herself in those terms. She thought of herself as a future engineer, one of those scientists people admire and respect and fall silent to when they speak.

---

Many of her friends worked part time here and there while in school. Some had jobs where they only worked nights. They'd come to class with their mascara smudged beneath their eyes and with a faraway look that, over time, coarsened into rough, cynical words and red lips. And the rougher and more cynical their words became, the brighter their lipstick became, the more their eyes darkened, the more a hatred of them deepened in some of their classmates.

Insults, from both girls and boys, began to follow them wherever they went. Rumor had it that a group of students had cornered one girl in the bathroom and beat her up so badly that she ended up in the hospital, and she never returned to school.

Ghalia's friends braved the abuse because they had access to a world that other students didn't, because they experienced things their classmates thought only existed on TikTok or Instagram, and because their illicit jobs brought them money they could give to their parents and to their little brothers and sisters.

"And besides," as one friend told Ghalia, "some have it worse than us. Like the boys who want to be with other boys, or the girls who are boys, or the boys who are girls. But the Africans have it the worst. They can't hide behind a veil or a beard or prayer because their skin color is who they are. It's an open invitation to slurs and disrespect, and worse."

Ghalia listened carefully. It wasn't like her to judge, or give her opinion on things she knew little about. Encouraged by Ghalia's thoughtful silence, her friend continued, as some other girls listened on.

"But don't think that threats against them, or us, or anyone who can't be like everyone else are just random. There's this organization that has a cell in the school. Not Islamists actually, but a pretty powerful group with ties to the police. They have informants here. How better to intimidate and control us, the unruly university students—the little brothers and sisters of those who were part of the Arab Spring twelve years ago? Their flunkies may look immature and stupid, and we tease and torment them; but they're backed up by a serious bunch, so we know who to steer clear of. And you should, too."

Some laughed, as though the fear that came through the girl's words was absurd. But they knew it wasn't.

Then her friend showed Ghalia the money she made, sometimes up to a thousand dirhams a night.

"Look, isn't it beautiful? Smell, the scent of freedom!"

It was more than what Ghalia made in one week.

She went on.

"With your long curly hair, your golden eyes and beautiful figure, you could make as much as we do, if not more. Granted, you're dark and men here like their women pearly white, but there's something about you…Plus, you're not veiled, you walk with confidence, and this is a public institution, not one of those fancy private ones. So, the opinions others have of you are already skewed. So why not do it? All your friends think you should. There are rumors that you're a maid. Nothing wrong with that. But you could become a star, a singer, or a dancer, fly to the Arab Gulf States, trick some wealthy Arab man into buying you a house in the home country and filling up your bank account—it's nothing for them. And you'd be rich and could take care of your parents and your sister. And when you're rich, trust me, no one cares how you made that money. You could be a queen, Ghalia, if you did that, instead of scrubbing floors till your breasts sag and studying for your exams till your eyes burn out."

"Or I could be disappeared in a trafficking ring and never heard from again," Ghalia responded.

"No, that only happens to Eastern European girls, not to us. We have it all. We understand these men, we're from the Orient. But we do things their wives don't even know about."

"I prefer to get my degree as an engineer and, maybe, find a job in Canada," Ghalia persisted.

They all laughed.

"You do that," she said. "We don't have half your brains. We need to have options."

"You know, it's not half bad working in a decent home," said Ghalia. "Bed and board, time away from my folks, the Internet, and quiet time. Sometimes, you make friends, even surprising ones."

There were nods of understanding, of grudging respect.

"But be careful—don't get too full of yourself. There's a price to pay when you're a proud woman. It's a deadly combination," came her friend's warning, bittersweet, between envy and genuine concern.

"And those thugs that pollute our halls, they hate you as much as they hate us," she continued, lowering her voice. "They hate you because you're smarter than them, and you don't even look at them. Be careful. Maybe they hate you even more than they hate us," were her parting words.

"Don't worry about me. I know what I'm doing, and where I'm going," said Ghalia.

But she didn't tell them everything. She had a secret of her own.

————✦————

Two in fact.

Jeanne Ba, the Senegalese housekeeper, known as Zahra, hadn't seen her family or country in over three years. Despite mutual prejudices and sometimes violence between Moroccans and immigrants from West Africa, Ghalia and Jeanne immediately felt at home with each other.

Both were reserved and quiet by nature, and found it easy to talk to one another. They shared common interests—how machines work, how to fix old, broken household appliances—and a passion for podcasts and documentaries about scientific discoveries and technological advancements, for which they sent links to one another on their phones. Jeanne helped Ghalia improve her French, and Ghalia shared her class notes and papers with her because you never know when they can come in handy. Even though their days ended late, at around nine, and started early in the morning, at six, they found stolen moments.

One day, a university colleague came to drop off an engineering manual that a group in the class shared during lockdown. It was Jeanne who opened the front door for him. After that, he came often to see her, until Amber put a stop to it. But Ghalia knew Jeanne continued to see the young man, Ali. She told her she was happy for her, that he was one of the good ones.

————✦————

Her other secret was her employer, Kamal.

At first, he had been distant, although always polite,

courteous even. His deep blue eyes looked elsewhere, never on her too long. Ghalia was used to men who stared, to men who didn't care if they made her uncomfortable by their staring.

She was surprised by the relationship Kamal had with his wife. They barely spoke, and they were intent on avoiding one another as much as they could. When they did exchange words, their communication seemed to have layers that Ghalia didn't understand and that further pushed them away from one another. She thought it must be because of their daughter, Al. The girl dressed like no one Ghalia knew, listened to strange music, then stopped talking, even though there was nothing wrong with her.

When Nadine Mesari asked Ghalia to come stay with them during lockdown, in March 2020, Ghalia felt a profound relief. She'd eat her fill, have a room she shared with Dada Amber, access to her courses, if and when they were put online, and a lovely garden. Most importantly, she'd be in the employ of a polite, though estranged, family and far from her own, difficult, invasive, and impoverished one.

At first, Kamal continued to be polite and distant, barely acknowledging her presence. He was an elegant man, even during lockdown. His jeans were well cut, and his t-shirts revealed muscles he worked hard to develop. She did notice—although it was fleeting and could have been her imagination—an underlying scent mingled with his perfume every time he passed near her. She couldn't describe it, but it was a scent that reminded her of overripe fruit, or meat almost gone bad, and oddly, it made her sad to tears. She had never met a man like him.

Time passed. Kamal asked her to bring his meals to his office. She noticed that the drawings on his desk resembled the technical blueprints she was being taught at university, but less technical. When he saw her interest, he offered to show her the plans for the project he was building.

"I'm working, but construction projects are stopped. And clients have stopped paying. I'm keeping my mind busy. It's easy to go insane, isn't it?"

He laughed as his blue eyes settled on her for the first time.

Ghalia hesitated, then looked back at him. His eyes were a deep blue, but they had a coldness. Their encounters were brief and formal, but daily. He spoke to her mind and never looked at her tall, strong body and rounded breasts.

Ghalia stayed up at night thinking of him, and her heart beat in anticipation at the thought of meeting him in the morning. She had never allowed herself to feel anything for a man. Though it would be hard for her friends to believe it, she had never been with a man before. And the reason was simple: she didn't want to be trapped in a relationship with a man who lacked ambition or in a marriage with children before she had reached her goals. She wasn't naive. She knew a relationship and children would put a stop to her dreams of becoming an engineer, of moving to Canada. And she wanted to be like those American women on the Internet with the beautiful suits and bank accounts. Some even had skin like hers and bodies like hers.

But with Kamal, she felt differently. Time passed, and his hand brushed hers. He didn't move it. He pulled up his sleeve, revealing the gold Rolex on his wrist and looked at the time, for no other reason than perhaps to show he was a busy man or that he owned a gold watch.

"You're different from other women."

She hesitated, then moved her hand.

"Ghalia, you're a strong, independent woman. You work for us, but I know you're serious about becoming an engineer.

I know you're going places."

She just looked at him.

"I can help you get there. I know people."

"Why would you help me, sir?"

"Because I believe in you. And I like to help young people pursue their dreams. You're not the first."

"The first?"

She was about to leave the room but he took her hand.

"I mean no disrespect. I haven't felt what I feel for you for anyone."

"You have a wife, a child."

"You've seen our relationship. Do we seem like a husband and wife to you?"

"I don't know what you want from me, but I can't give it to you. If this is a problem for you, I'll leave right away."

But she stayed where she was, and he smiled, the cold in his eyes turning to ice.

"I respect your strength, your pride. It's you I want, Ghalia. Your mind, your heart, all of you. My wife used to be like you once. Proud and tough, but curious and gentle. Now…"

"Now?"

"She's disappearing, isn't she? It's like my house is inhabited by a ghost. Or I'm the ghost."

He smiled at her, showing his perfect white teeth.

Ghalia moved away from him. She felt uncomfortable at the way he spoke of his wife. But she couldn't stop her heart from beating a little faster and her face from flushing.

"I'm sorry if I offended you. I was an unhappy man until you came. But with you, I'm a new man. You're my queen. And I'm not worthy of you."

Ghalia didn't know real people spoke this way. They did, in movies, but not in the new ones. In the old, black-and-white ones. She felt unique, seen, and even, yes perhaps, loved. She found Nadine beautiful, though distant, and she saw her as the perfect example of a wealthy man's wife. She didn't envy her, but Ghalia was flattered that a man married to a woman like Nadine would be interested in her and see her worth.

"Mr. Mesari, you're a married man, and a father. What you're saying isn't right."

"That's what I admire about you. Your decency, your integrity. What happens between us has nothing to do with my wife and child. You and I, we could have a chance at real happiness. But forget I said anything at all."

His words resonated with her. She was falling in love, and this was terrifying. Kamal leaned in and kissed her on the mouth. It was a soft, long kiss, and it stopped at exactly the right time. He let go of her.

"You're perfection."

Ghalia's heart was racing when she left the office.

---

Back in her room, that night, she knew she had fallen in love with him. But it was all going too fast. She wished their love would remain pure and untainted by the flesh, far from sin or cruelty to others. She resolved that a kiss was all she could give for a long time, before things were clear and their actions blameless. And so, for a time, Ghalia tried to avoid going into Kamal's office, and when she did, she would quickly clean up and leave. He didn't seem to notice her presence, or her absence.

Still, she began to look forward to seeing him every morning. She put particular care into the way she brushed her hair and knotted it underneath her headscarf, in the cleanliness of her uniform. She made up her eyes, for she knew that was the only part of a woman's face that can be made up carefully, without looking vulgar, just to enhance the color of the eyes and the curve of the lashes.

One day, Kamal looked at her and she was certain he smiled, but a discreet, half-hidden smile. Almost a sad smile, she thought. And that made her feelings for him deepen. He wasn't like the other men she knew. He respected her wishes, he respected her. He knew how to eat without making too much noise. And he had taste: he listened to instrumental music and followed a strict diet to maintain his body. She tried not to think of the ice in his eyes, or the overly sweet scent beneath the cologne. In all his gestures, except when the ice settled in his eyes, he seemed kind and good.

One day, she went in to clean the office, and he was sitting there, facing the window, looking at the sun streaming down onto the dried-up patches in the garden. He turned and looked at her. His eyes were of the lightest blue, cold as ice. And there was a smell, in the room, a sickly sweet, unbearable smell, that was stronger than before.

"Should I come back another time?"

"No, come in. You never bother me, you know that."

Ghalia walked in and began dusting the table, picking up the dirty coffee mug and breakfast tray. He got up, went behind her, and put his hands on her shoulders. She stopped what she was doing, but didn't move away. His hands then went around her neck, and she felt something cold and thin around it. The disturbing scent was there, near her neck.

"It looks beautiful on you."

She raised her hand to her neck and felt a thin, cold chain.

"No, I can't."

"Please, accept my gift. It belonged to my mother and is supposed to go to my wife or my daughter, but I want you to have it. I want you to understand what you mean to me."

He turned her around and kissed her on the mouth. She opened her mouth, but then his breath touched hers—sweet, oversweet, rotten sweet, fresh mint covering up an acrid taste. She closed her eyes. When the kiss became too insistent, she pushed him away. He pulled her back toward him.

"No," said Ghalia, "no."

"Don't be coy, it doesn't suit you. No one will find out. I know you want this as much as I do. I see the way you look at me. And you're important to me. More than anyone else. You're the only one who makes me feel alive. That means something."

Ghalia's world and illusions were crumbling like sand around her.

She hit him across the face.

He took a step back, stunned. His pearly white skin turned pink instantly. He put his hand on his cheek, and the ice in the blue of his eyes became a storm.

She thought he would hit her back, but he didn't. Instead, he made a strange, low sound almost like a growl, and told her to get out.

"You'll regret this little act you pulled," he said softly as she was leaving. "I don't lose."

———◦×◦———

Ghalia had been told that her pride and reserve could be mistaken for arrogance. How many times had she heard people complain about her. *Who the hell does she think she is?* was a phrase that had followed her most of her life. Though these words had made her feel lonely and misunderstood, they had never quite crossed over to be threatening. But there was something in the way Kamal said his words that turned her soul to ash.

She confided to Jeanne about her fears.

"If anything happens to me, know it's him. He did it to me."

"He's not a violent man. He's not like the men in our worlds."

"Jeanne, I've come to think that all men are capable of violence, if given the chance. Even the wealthiest, best-mannered ones. In fact, they may be the worst because they can hide what they do and people always forgive them everything."

"Being all stuck here together for all these months doesn't help. Could you go back to your family?"

"Covid has been hard on them. They're relieved I'm here. It means more space there and more food for the three of them. And the extra money I send them always helps. I pray all this passes before he does something."

Her late-night conversations with Jeanne, tucked away on the same bare mattress in Jeanne's room, were the only moments of comfort and ease Ghalia experienced these last months in the Mesari household.

⁂

One late night, almost at dawn, Ghalia woke up for her morning prayer. When she was done, and knowing she'd have to be up in an hour at most and unable to go back to sleep, she decided to go up into the house and get a glass of milk. On her way back down to her room, she heard some noise. She thought she saw Al in the shadows, but she must have been mistaken, for when she looked again, there was no one there.

She was turning back toward the staircase that led to her room when something solid pinned her against the wall. It was a man's heavy body. His breath, oversweet, awash in mint and alcohol, and rotten to the core, was impossible to mistake. He put his hand on her mouth, so she couldn't scream. She tried to break free, but he was too strong and she couldn't move. She stood there, pinned to the wall, crushed by his body, unable to breathe...

---

"There now, we're even," he said when he was finally done. "Don't you ever treat me that way again. I cared about you, I showed you respect, I told you I loved you. And I thought you did too. But you thought you could toy with me. Look what you made me do."

He backed off, zipped his pants.

"I'll be expecting my breakfast in an hour," he said.

And as he was leaving, he stopped and turned to her.

"I recommend you don't mention this incident to anyone, or try to leave the house in the middle of the pandemic. As you know, I'm highly connected, and it would be easy for me to make trouble for you." He took a deep breath. "You're better off here anyways."

---

That was the first time. And there were other times. But between the first time and the next, she called her mother. Though they weren't close, she needed her more than she ever had. She thought of calling her father, whose love she didn't doubt. But she was filled with shame and knew that he would never have the courage to shield her from her mother, from the neighbors, from the world.

"Mama."

"Yes, child."

"I'm in trouble."

Her mother's voice hardened.

"Did you lose your job?"

"No. But I can't stay here anymore. I need to come home."

Her mother turned shrill and wild.

"What did you do!"

"I'm in danger, Mama."

"In danger? What devil words are those? What did you do?"

"Please, I need to come home."

"We need that money, Ghalia. Think of your little sister, think of us. We let you study, but we need that money. Be a good girl."

"Yes, Mama."

"Whatever evil has come to you, know that a woman always has control over how others see her, and how they treat her. I was beautiful once too, and look, I didn't stray. I'm a respected wife and mother."

She paused, her voice both soft and hard, for she knew she had won the battle.

"It's up to you to be respected."

"Yes, Mama."

"Goodbye, child."

———— ❦ ————

For months, Ghalia didn't even tell Jeanne about what happened, not until her belly started showing.

"Help me," was all she could say.

"Oh, beloved, it's too late now. Why didn't you tell me before? There are ways."

"I didn't know. I can't keep it."

"There are signs," said Jeanne as Ghalia stared at her in silence.

"Was this your first man?"

"Yes."

"Was it…what you wanted?"

The shame was deep, tentacular. It spread through her body and soul like a poisonous weed.

"No."

"Could you ask him for help? If he is who I think he is, it's in his best interest that this situation…disappear."

"I can't ask him for help. I can't bear to even look at him."

Ghalia closed her eyes and pressed her face against Jeanne's chest, her warmth and her calm the only respite she had.

"How foolish I was, Jeanne. Thinking he loved me, thinking I loved him. This is all my fault."

"Women are raised in the dark. We're encouraged to be fools, victims of our own fantasies. But this is not your fault."

"My behavior triggered his."

"Oh, *ma petite chérie, si naive*. He's a professional," she kissed her hands, "and he made you think you could be queen."

"Help me."

"There are ways, but it's dangerous. You could die."

"What other choice do I have? What future now, for me, for…"

"There are women who have herbs that can get rid of it. But they are poison for both of you. And the bleeding that follows could be endless. And it might not stop until you're dead too."

"I have to do something."

"I'll try. I'll call some people. But it will cost you. They're not kind people. I know girls who had to deal with them." She hesitated. "You know, Amber has that knowledge stored in her brain and in her closets like an encyclopedia."

"That old witch. She'll never help."

"No, for sure. She'll make sure to kill you in the process."

Their laughter, low and soft, hid their fears.

"I bet she's killed in the past," Ghalia mused.

"Oh yes, those wrinkles hide many dark secrets."

———————

The next evening, a woman came to the gates of the Mesari household. She looked like a beggar, and her face was hidden under a cape. Jeanne told Amber she'd give the beggar woman a loaf of bread and some cheese, before telling her to leave.

Jeanne went to the front door. Food and killing medicine exchanged hands, and the old beggar woman left, her back straightening as she walked down the empty streets.

Jeanne heated water and poured in the herbs as instructed. She massaged Ghalia's stomach and lower abdomen with the oils and paste given to her by the angel maker.

Although Ghalia developed a high fever and was unable to work for the next two days, nothing else happened. A slight bleeding, and pain in the lower back for a week, were the only signs that Ghalia had tried to get rid of the thing inside her.

"It's not working. Maybe it's too late."

"Maybe that woman fooled us," said Ghalia.

"It's become very dangerous to help a woman ease her burden. What will you do?"

"What can I do?"

"Give it up for adoption."

"There's no adoption in this country, and an unmarried woman and her child end up on the streets. We'll be nothing. He won't have a name because he doesn't have a father."

Ghalia wrapped cloths tightly against her womb for as long as she could.

———————

Throughout those long months, only one other person discovered her condition: Kamal. One day, he pressed himself against her, his hand covering her stomach, and found that it was round and hard. There was anger in his voice when he spoke.

"What's this? Are you trying to trick me? Get rid of it."

"I tried."

"Whore."

There was panic in his voice.

"I know a doctor. He'll help you if I tell him to. He's used to…situations like these, to women like you. Go to him."

On her day off, Ghalia went to the doctor.

---

His office was clean and modern. He was soft spoken and gentle. His face was very white and his eyes colorless. He made her lie down and take her clothes off. He barely covered her nakedness with a surgical sheet. He listened to her heartbeat and pressed the cold gel against her belly before starting the ultrasound. He pressed hard and it hurt. His hands were cold and moist. Ghalia felt hot tears flow down her cheeks.

The doctor smiled.

"Mr. Mesari asked me to examine you and see what can be done. I'm always glad to help Mr. Mesari. He's a good man, and he doesn't like loose ends. But this time, it's too late. I can't do anything, even for him. You must know that situations such as yours, asking me to do what you want me to do, is illegal. I could lose my license. You're too big, too advanced. Tell him I can't help him this time. Now get dressed and get out. You're all paid for."

Ghalia returned to the Mesaris.

She had nowhere else to go, and she knew she would need to leave soon. She just needed a little more time to figure out her next move. When she arrived, Kamal called her into his office.

The stench was everywhere. How could she not have smelled it before? She felt weak.

"The minute it's here, throw it away. You wouldn't be the first woman to get rid of her problem this way."

Ghalia didn't respond.

"I don't need to explain to you what I can do to you if you don't take me seriously. Do you understand?"

But Ghalia didn't answer him.

"Sickly sweet, rotten and corrupt," was all she said.

Kamal shrank back in his seat.

"What did you say?"

"The smell, you must know it's there. You must smell it, no? No one has ever told you, not even your wife? But it's there, sir. You're not imagining it. It's there."

Kamal rose very slowly.

"Get out of my house."

---

Ghalia left the Mesari household. All she had with her was a scrap of paper on which was written the address of a women's center and the name of the woman who ran it.

But first, she tried to go home. The violence and rejection she encountered were deep and profound. When her time came, the birth didn't happen in a hospital or in a clinic. She was taken to a woman, known for these kinds of things, who once may have been a midwife, but who seemed to have forgotten the knowledge and compassion that came with her trade. She made her lie on a straw mat that smelled of terrible things and terrible doings. When the baby was born, she cut the umbilical cord and held him to her.

"Leave the baby with me," she told Ghalia. "It's a boy. No one will want him. I'll find something for him. And you'll get paid. Well, I mean you won't owe me for the birth."

Ghalia stared at the dirty fingers clutching her baby, turning his back blue. Despite her pain, she rose from the mat and slowly, but her eyes cold and steady, she took the baby away.

"No," she said.

She paid her and left.

⁓

When she went home, Ghalia knew she couldn't stay. There was no room for them. Where she had once lived, there was now only shame and hatred. A shame and hatred that swelled from her parents' house and spread into their neighborhood. And that turned into violence and danger. A kiss to her beloved sister, and then she left in the dead of night, with the Center's address burnt like gold in her memory.

⁓

The woman named Nayla who took her in was tough and kind. Ghalia stopped trembling the moment she opened the door for her, wide and ever-welcoming.

"Come in, come in. You and your baby are safe now. Come in from the cold," said Nayla. "Your new life begins here."

Ghalia and Noor entered the Center, leaving the darkness behind them, and all around them. A refuge in the midst of an endless storm.

# 19

# Jeanne

Jeanne, at barely twenty-five years old, was used to being alone. There were strong Senegalese communities in the city, and being among them could warm your heart, make you proud and ease your yearning for the home country. But there was also endless, obsessive talk of wooden boats to cross the Mediterranean, of orange life jackets as the only protection against storm and current, and of *passeurs*, those men akin to devils who hold your life in their hands and will let you drop to the bottom of the sea if the tide turns or if they see a bright red light and armed coast guards heading in their direction.

Jeanne decided, early on, that being among her own was an exercise in self-punishment and cruel fantasy. If and when she was ready to attempt the great crossing, she would turn to them. Till then, she would keep to herself. She needed to stay level-headed until she knew what her future bore her, what doors would open.

She shared a room in the neighborhood of Al Oulfa with five other West African women who, like herself, all worked in people's homes or in hotels. But they didn't see much of each other because they didn't have the same days off. And except for the rare times she joined them for an evening or an afternoon at the beach, she kept to herself. Besides, she sent whatever money she had to her mother and little brothers and sisters back in Senegal, and spent very little on herself.

---

Her first employers were a Moroccan couple living in a large house on the outskirts of Marrakesh. They were the ones who changed her name to Zahra.

"Our staff are ignorant locals. They don't like black skin and Africans, even though their skin is as black as yours, if not blacker—charcoal."

The employer shook his head.

"We'll call you Zahra, and they'll think you're Muslim, perhaps even a Moroccan from the southern oases whose Arabic is incomprehensible to them. And Zahra is a good, honorable Muslim name, since it's the name of the prophet's daughter, and also the name of a flower, and women with your skin color have traditionally been given the names of flowers in our country."

He finished with a soft smile.

Jeanne didn't stay long at their service. The other maids complained to their employers that she had a strong smell, that the food she cooked, though good, for she always shared it with them, also had a strong, unbearable smell. They wouldn't let her sleep with them in the room the female employees shared at the back of the house, behind the kitchen, because, they complained, her smell and snoring were overpowering.

One night, Jeanne walked down the long hallway that led to the back of the house to the servants' quarters and found that her mattress had been dragged out of the room and into the hallway. It was clear that she was expected to sleep there. When she asked the maids for her clothes and belongings, they said they didn't know where they were. Perhaps someone threw them in the trash, thinking they were trash because of their smell.

When the other maids understood that Jeanne wouldn't breathe a word to a soul or repeat the incident to their employers, they began keeping food from her and giving her barely enough to sustain her through the day. Scraps of the scraps they received from their employers, and the rice and okra she had cooked with such joy and shared with them with such pleasure, also disappeared.

Still, Jeanne kept quiet. She knew Moroccan employers believed their own and saw their West African maids as less than human, but also as creatures capable of great harm, of frightening witchcraft, poised on the edge of great dangers.

Later that week, Jeanne noticed her small locket, bearing the Virgin Mary, on one of the older maid's neck. She had learned to work hard and keep her mouth shut in this African country that was both white and black, familiar and estranging, Muslim and profoundly superstitious, a superstitious spirit that reminded her of ancient West African Voodoo, but that believed in its superiority as white, Arab, and Muslim.

But not this time.

She cornered the older maid in one of those endless, dirty hallways, prevalent in the Marrakesh villas built in the seventies, and which no one ever cleaned or complained about. She took off her head scarf, let loose her raven black hair, let free its shine and curls, watched the other woman's face fill with terror, and pushed her into the filthy wall.

"Give it back. Give it back or I'll have the she-demons of the night eat your liver and your heart while you sleep, and no one—not even you—will ever know why you're losing strength and slowly dying. Give it back you old hag, or you'll never know peace again."

Batoul, the older maid, stared at her in horror. There was a she-demon, right there, in front of her—black skin, jet black hair, black eyes, and curled, bird-like fingers. She had heard of the power of West African sorcerers, even though she herself had never used their black magic, only protective amulets and talismans with Quranic verses scribbled on the piece of paper contained inside. She unhooked the necklace from her throat and threw it at Jeanne's feet.

"Take it. It's worthless to me. I found it on the floor. I should have known this piece of junk belonged to you."

Jeanne knew that by terrifying the family's oldest and most reliable maid, a thief and a gossip, she had made an enemy. Still, she couldn't help but chuckle softly to herself at the other woman's sheer terror.

A few weeks passed, and the master of the house called her into the living room. The man sat on the couch in the center of the room. It was white vinyl with silver, eagle-like legs. While he spoke, she noticed for the first time that the vinyl was dirty and worn around the edges, and that the silver veneer on the bird-like feet, that had always intimidated her so, was peeling off, revealing the gray plastic beneath. She blinked and for the first time saw the house as it really was: old, pretentious, broke, and full of fear.

To her surprise, he wasn't cruel or spiteful. She even sensed a slight embarrassment in his attitude toward her.

"My grandfather, Hadj Ahmed, lived in Senegal. Did you know that? He made his fortune there, and he said that the black men were more reliable than the white men. They were eager to work and more honest than most. He said we were one great empire once. He understood you people. I think I get that from him. You're a hard worker, I have no complaints. But my wife, she…you must see this, you're a smart girl, she listens to her own, and we need peace in this house. You see that, don't you, it's not the most peaceful house, is it?"

He laughed nervously.

"They want you gone. But I have something for you. Friends of mine, in Casablanca, they agree to take you on. It will be a little more pay, so that should please you. It's not like you have much of a choice. It's that, right, or on the *patera* across the Mediterranean, right, with all your friends, down to the bottom of the sea."

Again, that nervous laugh.

This was the most kindness Jeanne had received since her arrival in Morocco two years ago. She didn't understand then why there was this harsh anger, this hopeless cry coming from deep within her body. Shouldn't she feel grateful?

She bit her lip and clenched her stomach to stop it from coming out. She nodded quietly and waited. He told her she could go and showed her the kitchen door with his hand.

"My passport, sir."

He stared at her and then a thin smile formed on his lips.

"Oh yes. Here you go. Here's the address. You can go straight to the train station. Kamal and Nadine Mesari. They're waiting for you."

She could see it wasn't easy for him to return her passport. Moroccan employers held the passports of their West African and Asian employees lest they chose to leave their employ and try their chance elsewhere. Most were in Morocco illegally, and this was a way for the employers, and the agencies that provided them with this cheap, foreign labor, to protect themselves.

Jeanne was, in effect, her employers' prisoner. If he didn't give her back her passport, she would have nothing left.

Her heart started beating. What if he decided to keep it? What would she do then? But, in the end, he gave it to her. He gave it to her slowly, hesitantly, the way one relinquishes a prized possession, a precious heirloom. Again, that wild howl and desperate anger deep inside her.

She quickly took it from his hand, took off the blue apron (which she knew the other maids would throw into the garbage), picked up her clothes, her bible, her brush, her shampoo, and her fake Versace perfume and left the house.

"My name is Jeanne, Jeanne Ba," echoed in the streets as she walked the long walk to the train station and got on the train that would take her to Casablanca, three hours away.

———⊱⋅⋅⋅⋅⋅⋅⋅⋅⋅⋅⊰———

Jeanne had been in Nadine's and Kamal's service for a little over two years, and the Mesaris planned on her one day replacing Dada Amber for the cooking as well as the cleaning she already took on. But, after a year in their service, their daughter Al fell to a strange illness and Jeanne was asked to take care of her.

Though Jeanne became more and more certain that one day she would leave, that she too would try the *great crossing* and leave Africa, its fears and its enslavements, behind, she wasn't ready yet. She hadn't enough money or courage or contacts, yet. And there had been only one time when she thought she could stay. One moment when she thought she could pause and build a life there, and even be loved and have a husband and children there, like other women did.

———⊱⋅⋅⋅⋅⋅⋅⋅⋅⋅⋅⊰———

The Mesaris were kinder than their friends, her previous employers. More modern, as they liked to repeat. At least, they tried to behave fairly toward her, as fairly as an Arab employer might treat an African employee in North Africa. They would say please and thank you, and tell the other servants to be respectful and polite toward her. They told their daughter Al that she was lucky that Jeanne could speak to her in French, and even a little English, and Wolof, and she would tell her fabulous stories of Africa, whereas Moroccan caretakers only spoke Arabic, and most preferred the Berber of their villages. What use was that language in the modern world? And who better than the Mesaris to know it was a useless language, for their ancestors on the paternal grandmother's side, the great Ahensals, had once been one of the most powerful Berber tribes in the kingdom, and they didn't speak Berber.

Jeanne didn't feel anything toward the Mesaris. Neither resentment nor gratitude, love nor hatred. They were kind enough, but more as a matter of image, she thought, than actual kindness. After all, her employers' true souls, their deep-seated prejudices and disgusts, were still unknown to them, and they perhaps would never know what they were truly capable of, what evil, what doubt, what fear. Sometimes Jeanne would get a glimpse of their souls: they didn't want her touching their food or their plates, they asked that she never use their daughter's bathroom, even on those nights that were difficult for Al, so Jeanne would sleep in her room; and they would discretely spray air freshener after she'd left the dining room.

Moroccans were a strange people: their skin was sometimes the same color as hers. Yet they still showed disgust at her appearance and some called her *abid*—slave—to her face. As for employers, even hers, she sensed that they took a certain pride in having West African servants, and sometimes confided in her that it reminded them of their childhoods, their great-grandparents' formidable homes and their troops of slaves, the Dadas who had raised their parents and their parents' parents. She knew this because she heard them say so to their friends. Heard them wax nostalgic that they missed their days as slave masters. Bragging, was more like it.

The older servant, Dada Amber, was polite enough most of the time, but she didn't want Jeanne there. And Jeanne suspected that was why, once again, she didn't share her room with her and Ghalia.

But Ghalia, she was different. Even so, Jeanne kept to herself at first and took care of Al, her room, her clothes, her daily walks in the Park Murdoch. She read to her, brought her food, knew what music to play, and when to turn the lights off. What would happen to Al if Jeanne left? What would happen to Jeanne if Al was cured?

Jeanne had been quick to map out the situation at the house. There was Dada Amber, who claimed she was related by blood to the lady of the house, though her black skin reflected Jeanne's own, but paler, as though a sudden wind had raised the desert sands and spread the grains onto her ebony skin, like flickering gold dust. And there was Ghalia, the young maid, who had arrived close to two years ago, who was kind and eager to learn.

There was also a gardener, Bouchaib, who would come twice a week, but who didn't take his job seriously and let half the garden dry out and get overwhelmed by weeds, and whom Amber hated with a deep-seated, irrational hatred, to the extent that she barely gave him water on hot days.

Even though Jeanne kept to herself, Ghalia was nice to her. It even seemed that she wanted to be friends.

At first, Jeanne thought Ghalia was playing a trick on her, pretending to be kind in order to humiliate her. But in fact, Ghalia was genuinely interested in her. Jeanne tried to find in her the disgust and resistance she had encountered countless times since her arrival in Morocco. But not once could she doubt Ghalia's intentions. She was transparent and crystal clear. This woman was naturally good.

In halting French, Ghalia told her that she was at university and trying to learn that language. She also told her that, while studying, she had met students from West Africa—Senegal, Mali, Ivory Coast.

"They're my friends," she said. "They help me with my French, sometimes even a little English. If it weren't for them, I wouldn't feel comfortable speaking French. I teach them Arabic in return," Ghalia explained, smiling at Jeanne.

Jeanne would simply nod and keep to herself. Until one day. Ghalia asked her a more personal question.

"Please tell me, I have a friend, Jean-Baptiste, he's from Senegal, like you. He said to ask you if your real name is Zahra," said Ghalia and she laughed, as though this suggestion were absurd.

Jeanne didn't respond immediately.

"Why does he want you to ask me that?"

"He said many employers here change their Christian maids' names to Muslim names, because they sound better."

Jeanne hesitated, and after looking at the other woman's clear eyes and frank smile, she answered.

"My name is Jeanne," she replied, as relief swept over her, and she struggled to keep her eyes dry. She was surprised to see tears in Ghalia's eyes, too.

"Then I'll call you Jeanne, from now on."

And the two women smiled at each other.

"How cruel it must be for you, what you must feel. My grandmother named me Ghalia—it means 'precious.' I was precious to her as a child, even if girls aren't precious here. She would pray for my mother to have a son, but only to protect me. But she never did. My mother only had another daughter, my younger sister. Yasmina."

"Does this worry you?" asked Jeanne.

Ghalia nodded, then she continued.

"My mother never cared about us, not like my grand-mother did. It's like I could only disappoint her. I don't have a brother. If I did, we'd be protected. We'd keep our apartment if anything happened to my dad. But, because we don't have a brother, our apartment would go to my dad's nearest male relative, and we'd be out in the street. It made my mom bitter, but it made me want to work. I'm good at school and I study hard. In the meantime, I have to do this kind of work in the summer or when school is off, to pay for food and books, and I try to save a little for later. But it doesn't bother me much, work doesn't scare me. Plus, it's room and board. I want to work. I want to go places. What does Jeanne mean?"

Jeanne started laughing.

"Jeanne is the name of a saint. A saint who stood up to men, made war on kings and then was burned alive, like a witch. Jeanne d'Arc. She was French."

She noticed Ghalia's shock.

"What a name to carry…"

"Look, there are worse things than having your name changed. There's forgetting your name and who you are and where you're from. And that, I pray I never do."

They stared at each other, sharing an instant understanding, and fear.

When Ghalia heard that Jeanne had also wanted to be an engineer, she showed her the books and papers they used.

"There's also some math and some statistics. Maybe you'll enjoy them."

And while Jeanne did enjoy seeing a schoolbook again, looking at formulas and demonstrations, it was also too painful, for it reminded her of all she had lost.

Ghalia and Jeanne shared these moments sitting in the back courtyard. In that way, that summer close to two years ago, Jeanne made her first friend. And that is how she met him, Ali. And how she began to think that it would be possible for her to live in Casablanca, with him, until darkness overtook their lives.

<hr />

The maids' quarters were down the stairs and off the courtyard, where they hung the laundry to dry when the sun was hot and high in the sky. Dada Amber and Ghalia slept in one room. They had their own TV and a bathroom. Amber had shown Jeanne where she was to sleep. It was a storage room, with a Turkish bathroom, separate from their room.

"We don't want any trouble here," Amber grumbled.

*You fool,* thought Jeanne. *Your stolen ancestors may have come from the same place I do, or a nearby village or tribe. Maybe we're even cousins but you don't see anything beyond these walls that are your grave. You know nothing of what was stolen from you.*

Her room was cold and bare, but Jeanne was satisfied with it. Having a room all to herself, she could rest and assemble little trinkets from discarded coils and plastics, a hobby she had always enjoyed and that had prompted her teacher to tell her she should become an engineer. Her room had a signal, a weak one, but enough for her to send WhatsApps from the old phone she had fixed up, to her mother, brothers, and sisters in Senegal. She told them stories about Morocco, how rich the people were there, how plentiful their food and water, but also how lazy, how dirty, how superior they felt. Her family would all chuckle and click their tongues in wonder.

"It's like Europe, already. It could be. But it's the dark side of the mirror. Everything is tainted here. They don't know they're Africans. They don't even know they're black."

And there were chuckles and clickings of tongues.

But Jeanne didn't tell her mother that her employers had changed her name from Jeanne to Zahra. It would surely break her heart. When Jeanne first told her she had to leave Senegal, her mother had stopped talking for thirty days and thirty nights.

---

In Senegal, Jeanne had been a bright student, at the top of her class. Her teacher, a Canadian preacher, a woman with a rare desire to do good, had repeatedly spoken to her father and mother to let Jeanne pass the national exams to enter university. She could, she was certain, pass them and even get a scholarship to study in Dakar, be an engineer, have a future, help their family, even.

But Jeanne's father always refused, and Jeanne had left school to work for a family in the nearest town, cleaning and washing for them, and bringing home much needed money. Her mother, she knew, never forgave her father for his decision, and she turned away from him, day and night, until, exasperated and intent on revenge, he left them for another woman and other children.

When Jeanne told her mother she would leave the country and find work in northern Africa until she could find a crossing to Europe, that the money would help feed and raise the little ones, her mother's heart and tongue went dry and quiet for a month. Her bright, beautiful daughter on the pitiless desert roads, in a foreign country said to be cruel and unforgiving.

The mother also knew that one day, soon, the little ones would follow the eldest. That one after another they would go, and as surely as the earth turns around the sun, as surely as night follows day, she would lose them all, one after the other, to the great road and its unfathomable dangers.

So Jeanne kept her shame from her mother, and she whispered her name, her mother's name and the little ones' names in the dead of night, as though she feared she would forget them all, that her memory, too, would be taken from her.

She had never felt this lonely and this unseen in her life. Her friendship with Ghalia came as an unexpected, and welcome, gift.

———— ❦ ————

Jeanne had learned not to trust Moroccans, to quickly read in their eyes their disdain and disgust. It was never so with Ghalia. Jeanne had yet to see in her limpid eyes any sign of disdain or disgust. It became easy for her to let her guard down and see Ghalia as a fellow human being rather than a threat built around centuries of fear, subjection, and miscomprehension.

Jeanne also appreciated that Ghalia worked as hard as she did, and did the same tasks as she did without flinching or pretending or letting her do the filthy bits, while she stood by looking at her phone, like other Moroccan cleaners she worked with. They changed sheets together, cleaned dirty bathrooms together, flushed toilets when Kamal or Nadine forgot—they, who were always so impeccably dressed and flawlessly mannered. She and Ghalia picked up dirty underwear, and Jeanne wondered at the shamelessness of the rich. She would never let anyone see her dirty underwear nor dream of having anyone wash them. But they didn't seem to mind at all, and she understood that it wasn't only shamelessness. It was also that they didn't care what she, or Ghalia, or any maid, thought of them.

Sometimes, she'd find evidence of Kamal's doings with other women, and she would wash those too, and, after some time, she wouldn't let Ghalia see or clean those, because it seemed to cause her too much pain and fear.

They'd wash dirty dishes, and there, too, she'd wonder at how sloppy their employers were. The Mesaris had the perfect china, silverware, crystal glasses, flowers for great occasions. Lately, because they were a fashionable family, they had more earthy, brown-toned porcelains. But they never finished their food and let whole meals go to waste. She remembered how her mother struggled to put food on their plates, hers and her younger brothers' and sisters', and the anxiety on her face when they cleaned their plates too quickly and the eternal question she asked herself but never asked them, because there was nothing she could do about it: "Are they hungry? Did they eat enough? Are they going to bed hungry? Are they hurting?"

The Mesari's food would sometimes go to waste. For they didn't always allow the help to eat the remains, lest there was confusion in the household and the housekeepers began to eat their lobster, truffle pasta, prepared cakes and fancy exotic fruit, without permission.

Yet, there were aspects of her life that Jeanne was grateful for.

The first one was Ghalia.

And then there was looking after Al.

Surprisingly, Al always made sure her room was clean enough and her underwear washed before letting Jeanne pick up her clothes, wash the floors, or change the sheets. She would even, despite Jeanne's protests, pick up the mop, make Jeanne sit on her bed and clean the room. Al did so for no good reason, or no reason Jeanne could figure out, but it seemed to please her, to make her happy, having Jeanne sit on her bed while she cleaned.

Jeanne chuckled and clicked her tongue. It had to be to shock her parents and their picture-perfect lives that hid greater filth and dirt than anything she dusted and cleaned in Al's room. Sometimes, Al would leave the door ajar, hoping one of them would pass by, and Jeanne would quickly close it—the unspeakable, unacceptable swap of roles hidden inside. But Jeanne began to see that, in reality, though Al was quiet as a mouse, it gave Al peace of mind to work and clean her room, and help Jeanne, whom she liked, despite never telling her so.

And then there was the rare flip side. The unexpected breaks.

---

One day, the family traveled together and the help was given a few days off.

Amber never left the house, even when it was her turn to go out. She would leave, just for a couple of hours at most, to run errands or buy sweets she could only find in the souk at a certain merchant's stall. Once though, Jeanne recalled, she took a week off and went to Marrakesh to bury someone, though they never found out who it was. When Amber returned, she was silent for days and kept to herself.

Ghalia seized the opportunity. She invited Jeanne to come with her to meet her friends from university.

"They're not as smart as you are, but you'll like them," said Ghalia about her friends, intertwining Jeanne's fingers with hers. "But I promise, *chérie*, you'll have fun. It'll be a welcome change from the work you do every day and the people you see."

Jeanne got ready in her room. She oiled her hair and skin with a mixture of argan oil, shea butter, and floral scents made by a local Senegalese woman who understood that young women wanted their hair and skin to smell like perfume, and not like oil, the way their mother's skin smelled. Jeanne then braided her hair closely to her scalp and pulled it up into a high bun, to which she then attached a braided wig. She put black eyeliner under her eyes to enhance their depth, a smudge of pink lipstick on her lips, gold highlighter on her high cheekbones, and gold-plated hoops in her ears. She wore a long, blue-and-green, silk printed skirt, a black crop top, and brown sandals. She covered her shoulders in a blue-and-green printed shawl and was ready to go.

She hailed a taxi to take her to the popular juice and sandwich place on the corniche where she was to meet Ghalia and her friends.

———※———

Ghalia was sitting with a group of young people their age, early twenties, and she smiled and waved at her when she saw her. She introduced Jeanne to her friends, boys and girls, Moroccan and, to her surprise, West Africans. It was a cool, sunny spring day, which, in the past couple of years, had become a rare occurrence, as the winter months had turned hot and dry, and rain only appeared belatedly, during the harvest, in the months of March and April. But today, the weather was aligned for an easy, sunny get-together.

With Ghalia and her friends, Jeanne felt like a normal young adult. Not a migrant. Not a maid. Not a woman. Not Christian. Not poor. Not black. Just normal. She looked around the table at the smiling young faces. When a young woman from the Ivory Coast, Fatou, asked her what she did, she didn't know how to answer. Ghalia answered for her, laughing.

"She's my colleague. But she's smarter than all of us put together. She looks at a page in our textbooks and she right away knows it all by heart. Don't be fooled by her current job."

"She's the reason you started acing your classes, then!" laughed a pale young man with a long afro and colorful pants and t-shirt.

*Funny*, thought Jeanne. *They despise us, yet they try so hard to look like us. To be cool.*

She chuckled.

"What's so funny, genius?" asked a young woman with a rounded face, red lips, and heavily made-up eyes and eyebrows.

"It's just nice being out, breathing in the fresh sea air," said Jeanne, in her calm, quiet way.

As the evening progressed, she began to notice details about Ghalia's friends. She could tell by the way one young man discreetly counted the dirhams in his jeans, that some of them were poor, maybe as poor as she was. A couple of the women were heavily made up, with tight jeans, low-cut blouses, and high heels. But they had headscarves hidden in their bags, ones that they would quickly put on again when they went home or if they were stopped by an overzealous policeman.

Finally, the West African men and women who mingled with them dissociated themselves from the migrants begging on the street in plain view.

"That's not the same thing, you know. They don't come from the same places as us," one said.

But then, fear would sometimes crawl into their eyes as they looked away from the street to not be reminded that they could slide from one status to another in an instant, erasing the difference between themselves—international students who came to learn finance, engineering, medicine—and those poor migrants on the street, their children on their backs, hands outstretched, a distinction already invisible to many locals. It was a fate all too possible if they also decided, like some of their fellow students, that after university in Casablanca, they didn't want to go home, but stay in Morocco and look for a way to leave the continent.

Only one young woman, a Senegalese from Dakar who was in Casablanca to study medicine at the University, didn't seem to share their fears or their apprehensions. A couple of local young men, with long, sun-bleached hair and a surf-board on their shoulders, stopped at their table to chat with her. When Jeanne asked her how she knew them, the young woman, who went by the name of Lili, told her they surfed together.

"Surfed?"

"Yes, surf," laughed Lili. "Don't you know about surfing? Morocco is a surfer's paradise, just like Senegal."

"Do you surf here?"

"Here, in Agadir, Taghazout, Dakhla. I chase the waves down the Atlantic Coast. Some of the most beautiful coastline in the world, like ours, in Senegal. You're from Senegal too, yes?"

Jeanne nodded.

"One day, I'm going to drop my medical studies and open a surf camp with my surf buddies somewhere down south and live the life," said Lili. "And you're going to come see me and learn how to surf. With a body like yours, it'll be easy for you."

Jeanne stared. She didn't know it was possible to have fun in Morocco, with locals, men at that, on the beach. She didn't sense any discrimination from the young surfers who came to talk to Lili. Only the simple joy of a shared passion.

---

The sun had already set on the horizon behind the last wave on the western Atlantic shore, and spread pink, red, and yellow as far as the eye could see, when Ali joined them. He had a wide, innocent smile and the kindest eyes Jeanne had ever seen. His eyes set on her and, for the rest of the evening, he couldn't take them off her.

"Is there something on Jeanne's face, Ali?" teased one of the girls with the red lips and heavily made-up eyes, her arm playfully on his.

His eyes twinkled.

"Just the most beautiful eyes in the world," he said and laughed.

He then changed seats to sit next to Jeanne.

"If I may?"

He was one of those people whose candor and inner beauty shined through, and one only had to be near him to believe that this was true, that his presence was filled with grace.

Jeanne's connection with Ali was instantaneous, starlit, filled with joy.

He was a graffiti artist, a musician, and a songwriter. His artist name was Ard, Arabic for *Earth*. He went to school, but only because he wanted a degree, just in case. Jeanne got the impression that he was starting to make a name for himself in international circles, but he didn't brag. He just smiled shyly, watching her expression.

"I look at a broken-down wall and see possibilities," he said. "I paint the cracks and fissures, and the coolest wild beasts come out. In my music, I write what I feel and see—the struggles of my friends, my peers, the pain of the little kids who roam the streets at night. But also the joys—dancing, the football games, walks in the medina at night when the police are half asleep on the rooftops. I even got together a little collective where artists can come and work freely. Work is my life. At least it was, until now."

"Why? What happened?"

"You happened. I met you."

He held her hand and kissed her cheek, not seeming to care what anyone else around saw or thought.

But they cared.

The sky darkened and a chill blew past them.

---

Jeanne felt cold. Suddenly, it was difficult for her to breathe.

A group of young men approached them. As they came closer, Jeanne felt a despair, like a mother's wail.

In one of the city's harshest dialects, one of them spoke.

"Look at you all. Impure, dirty. Arab mingling with black, whores with men who aren't really men, Muslims with Christians. Your punishment is coming. You're angering the wrong people. We've got our eyes on you. You must have heard what we do to trash like you. The bee smoker,

*L'Enfumoir,* is in your future."

One of them stepped up to Ali, his eyes a black line.

"You for sure, watch yourself," he said, glancing at Jeanne. "Playing in dirt."

Ali stared back, barely containing his anger.

The group of young men left just as suddenly, leaving a blast of cold in their wake.

"What is L'Enfumoir?" Jeanne asked.

Everyone looked away. No one would answer. Finally, Matt, who was from the Ivory Coast, spoke up.

"It's a jail, a torture chamber for crimes that are only crimes in the minds of sick individuals like those boys."

"But no one knows for sure if it's a real place or just another way to try to scare people," Ali said. "Those guys don't like to see happiness."

"I have friends who have disappeared," said Matt, fear and fury rising in his voice. "I've heard it's a slave market. They sell women, children, blacks like me, for the best price, which is never very high, and you never see them again. My friends were warned first by gangs like that one. They feed on migrants, refugees, abandoned women and their kids, university students. They always sniff around folks like us," he said, gesturing to Jeanne, to the other West Africans, the heavily made-up woman, and to Ali himself. "He threatened *you too,* my friend. You're not immune."

Jeanne, who had kept a cool head throughout, turned to Ali.

"He didn't exactly threaten you, did he, Ali? It's like," she hesitated, "he was warning you."

Ali remained quiet while the others jeered loudly and vehemently.

"She's right. I know that boy. His name is Hassan."

"What happened to him?" asked Jeanne.

"A violent father who left him and his mother when he was young. He had to take care of his mother. He dropped out of school and started hanging out with guys like them."

"You feel bad for him?" asked Jeanne, more curious than surprised.

"I do, but he's still dangerous, even if he tried to warn me."

Ali turned to Jeanne, and his bright, joyous smile dispelled the lingering doom.

"But he's telling me to stop doing something I really like doing and that I'll never stop doing."

"What is that?" she asked, but she already knew, because she felt the same way.

"Being next to you."

⸻ ⬦ ⸻

Jeanne and Ali had a few endless, perfect weeks together.

Then one day, she received a phone call from an unknown number. She picked up the phone and heard a rough breath on the other end.

"We have your friend. If you want to see him again, come to *l'Enfumoir.*"

Jeanne's happiness crumbled.

"Yes. Just don't hurt him. Where are you?"

"Oh, we might hurt him a little, just as we might hurt you a little," the voice cackled. "But you'll take the risk now, won't you. You love him so much."

"Where do I go?"

"It's not too far. Enter Ouled Taieb Street and we'll send a messenger to get you through."

"I will."

"Hurry up, before it's too late."

The caller hung up.

———◆◇◆———

Jeanne stared at the ceiling for long minutes before turning off her phone. She did her chores as usual, took care of Al, kept her company, cleaned up, washed the dishes, and went to bed. The next morning, she woke up, washed her face, brushed her teeth, and went about her day.

She did this for a full week until, one morning, she turned on her phone again. And when she did, she saw the video they sent her of Ali's death. Underneath it was a caption.

"Your turn soon."

Jeanne's body shook, it was a deep, uncontrollable tremor. Her body broke into a thousand pieces from the stark images of Ali's ordeal.

Ghalia came into the room. She looked at Jeanne, then at the phone in her hands. She took the phone from her, looked at the video and understood.

"They would have killed you, too."

"He died alone. I wasn't brave enough to go to him. I abandoned him."

"It was a trap. He wouldn't have wanted you to come. I know Ali. He understood."

"He was alone. I left him there to die, alone."

Jeanne couldn't stop shaking. Her teeth shook, her eyes shook, her cheeks and her hair shook.

Ghalia held her close, wrapped her in her arms, rubbed her to bring back warmth.

"They would have done much worse to you than they did to him. Don't blame yourself. You lived a great love, with a man worthy of it, of you. And so did he. Very few are lucky enough to have what you two had," said Ghalia as she held her close. "See, my belly, filled by my violator. At least, you've known goodness and love, even if briefly. And so has he."

But whatever Ghalia might say, Jeanne would never be the same. She had abandoned a person she loved.

Was it out of cowardice, selfishness, pragmatism?

When Ghalia ran away from the Mesari household and found refuge in the center for single women and their illegitimate children, Jeanne knew, without doubt, that Ghalia would never be safe. The dreaded boys knew where Ghalia and she lived, and what they did.

And when Ghalia stopped sending her messages and replying to hers, she believed that she too would end up in *L'Enfumoir*. That soon, she too would be taken there to live out her days in darkness and fear.

# 20
# Al

Ever since she was a little girl, Al wanted to be like her mother. Her slender, blonde, elegant mother. And when people asked her if the beautiful woman with her was her mother, and if she was indeed Moroccan, being so blonde and white and slender, she would proudly answer, "Yes, and she's a doctor. She saves babies."

Al, however, was neither slender nor blonde nor elegant, and she saw herself just the way others saw her: her mother's less beautiful, less accomplished, less everything, daughter.

She had curly black hair that fell to her shoulders, pale skin, and dark brown eyes that, she believed, reflected no light or charm. But Al didn't mind since she loved and admired her mother more than anything in the world.

The more attached she became to her mother, however, the colder and more distant her mother became. It was as though her mother was annoyed by the intensity of her daughter's attachment, rather than being touched and moved by it. Her mother would regularly push her away, tell her she was busy, or lock herself up in her room. "Later, child. It's not suitable for a little girl to be so clingy," she'd say. And yet, Al had nowhere to go but to her mother's, and despite her mother's continued coldness toward her, she couldn't stop wanting to be near her, to smell her, to hold her. Al would stay as quiet as possible, move as little as possible, breathe as silently as possible, so that her mother would allow her to stay close to her.

When Al turned thirteen, and her body and desires began to transform, she also underwent a deeper, though invisible, transformation. Her intense attachment to her mother became anxiety and anger. She began to understand, though it was too difficult for her to fully admit it, that her mother kept her at a distance. She didn't return her embraces with the same warmth, she didn't spend time with her, nor ask about her day, nor, she realized, had she ever prepared her bath for her, or fed her, or dressed her. Especially after the death of the little brother.

From that moment on, her mother became withdrawn and barely laid eyes on her. Sometimes, she'd look at Al with fixed, unblinking eyes, and Al would wonder if her mother was imagining, wishing even, that it was she who had died instead of the little boy. Al didn't scream, or cry, or inquire about her mother's love for her. Instead, after all those years as a little girl learning to keep as still and quiet as she could, she kept still and quiet.

---

Al turned to her sketchbooks and to her pencils, to the sketching of imaginary worlds and creatures. She repeated the following words to herself, over and over again: *My mom doesn't like me.* And she would draw, painstakingly, meticulously, with three different crayons, in her notebooks.

After the little brother's death, it was clear to Al that the house she lived in would never be a home again and that her parents were an estranged couple. Her parents barely spoke to her or showed any interest toward her. She became restless. And the pencils and notebooks were no longer enough to soothe her loneliness or dampen her anger. She wasn't a child anymore. At least, she didn't consider herself a child anymore.

She had discarded the naivete, the endless love, the innocent adoration, for briefer, rougher, and easier pursuits and sensations—the thrill of danger, of the forbidden, the illicit. She began to hang out with a fast crowd and experiment with all kinds of drugs and sexual activity. She forgot her mother's cold, perfect face and her father's lengthening absences. Nobody explained to her about her body's transformations, and her lotus-like desires, both fruit and flower.

She learned about herself by seeing and doing, by being hurt and by hurting others. She put herself in danger and was excited by it. She binged. She kissed one and all, uninterested in either their sex or gender, driven only by the pain she saw in their eyes. That pain was a familiar one. She realized she enjoyed being with girls and with boys, but had a slight preference for girls with a very specific type. Cold, blonde, slender girls who looked at her with derision but gave her what she needed. But in times of loss and confusion, her recourse was always the same, though it wasn't her sole sustainment anymore: she'd take out her pencils, place them in front of her, from thinnest to thickest, and sketch in her sketchbook. Bodies intertwined to form many-headed creatures, urban decay exploding into blooming flowers, concrete walls into glass sculptures that were portals to other worlds.

One day, as she sat sketching in the brand new, ultra-modern Casa Finance City park, a young woman approached her.

"You're talented."

"I don't know."

"I do. You should do this more seriously."

"Why do you care?"

"I don't. But I'm an artist myself. I can't let sketches like that go to waste."

Al looked up from her sketchbook.

"Not wasted. They're in my sketchbooks. They're safe here."

"Sorry, let me rephrase that. I can't let a person who sketches like that go to waste."

Al fidgeted uneasily, and the young woman, whose name was Dina, sat down on the bench next to her. She had cropped red hair, and a strange, indescribable tattoo of a black cloud, thin and wispy, crawled across her left arm to just under her ear, where its final, smoky-gray strand nestled into the small of her neck, a volatile Adam's apple. She took the sketchbook from Al's hands and started turning the pages.

"Hey, you can't do that!"

Dina turned to her. Her eyes were outlined in black eyeliner—as black as the tattoo crawling up her arm, making their deep, intense green even deeper and more intense. *Poser*, Al thought, surveying her face.

"From up close, you're younger than I thought," said Dina. "You can't just do *this*. It's fun for a while, but you'll get lost doing nothing. Come with me."

———

With Dina, Al discovered an underground, an under-the-radar Casablanca subculture of hip-hop, slam, graffiti art, and urban dance. She took her to a space called The Factory, a converted slaughterhouse where musicians, dancers, and artists converged and shared their art and experiences. It was a hidden and unknown space, managed by a group of artists, videographers, and benefactors, both local and international, that gravitated around Dina and called itself the Factory Collective.

Al didn't know why these people did what they did. She didn't believe adults ever did things selflessly, but the energy of the place and the artists who congregated there were hard to resist.

She met girls and boys who were different from the kids she had known before, and who didn't even know that people like her parents, privileged and miserable, existed. Nor did they care. They knew there were "rich folk," and they knew there was little chance they would ever get to be one of them. But their world was so far removed from Al's parents' world that they didn't, wouldn't, dwell on it. Politics held no interest to them because they didn't believe it could change a thing. They resisted in other ways—through art, music, dance, strange dress codes. The girls were the most surprising to her. They didn't try to be beautiful or sweet, they wanted to be respected for their art and taken as seriously as the boys, especially in male-dominated scenes like hip-hop, slam, or graffiti art.

And so, between the ages of fifteen and sixteen, Al discovered more about her city and its hidden, endangered diversity than she had her entire life. She understood, confusedly and admiringly, that the kids around her were fighting for their survival, that they knew that if they couldn't express themselves freely, then the space they had so painstakingly carved from the rubble of urban, social, and educational decay would close up again, as though it had never existed.

She made friends with girls who would wear the veil on

their way home to their family's bidonville in obedience to its rules, but when they came back to the Factory, would hide it in their coat and dance or slam with their very souls.

She also met people like her, who drew and sketched manga-like figures in their sketchbooks that reflected imaginary worlds but also real, daily struggles. A monstrous giant taking the bread from a little guy, only to see the little guy transform into a powerful God, a machine rolling over a scared puppy only to have the puppy transform into water and drown the machine, a couple bent over a flower only to better share, and hide from the world, their kiss and their love…

---

Dina was always there, surrounded by younger boys and girls, teaching them and lecturing them. Her red hair was aflame and her piercings gleamed as she moved back and forth, talking and sketching, demonstrating and exposing. She had words that she used over and over again, like mantras: *diversity, resistance, freedom, modernity, creativity, art*… There was no denying her genius. Or her charisma.

At first, Al was skeptical, just as she was of most adults and authority figures. But, as she observed her and the pull she had on the younger artists, Al found it difficult to resist her. In fact, she became inexplicably drawn to her.

Dina barely acknowledged her presence and never complimented her art, though Al had never given so much of herself or worked so hard to do good and please someone.

"Stop trying to please me," Dina would scold her. "This isn't about me, it's about you. Look deep into yourself. Find your own voice. You have to grow up, Al. But don't lose your innocence, your freshness."

And Dina smiled, her white teeth pointed and bright like fangs in the moonlight, as she touched Al's cheek with a gnawed fingertip.

Al nodded and worked even harder.

———————

But Dina was never satisfied. No matter how hard Al worked, or the sacrifices she made—ignoring schoolwork, skipping classes, parties with friends, getting into trouble with parents and teachers—Dina repeated the same thing: "Look harder, go deeper. Stop trying to please me."

One day, a fellow artist at the Factory, thin and gaunt, approached her.

"Your work is wild and free," he said kindly. "But in a meaningless, disconnected way. I don't know what you're trying to do or say. But I can tell you this. Be careful with Dina. She's not who you think she is."

Al searched his eyes, surprised.

"What do you mean?"

The young man, whose name was Ali, looked at her sadly, and with fear in the folds of his irises.

"You feel it. You must."

Soon after, Ali stopped coming to the Factory. When Al asked Dina about him, she merely smiled.

"He's nothing," she said, grasping Al's chin in the palm of her hand. "He could have been something, but he didn't rise. This place isn't for everyone. Not everyone makes it. Only the best rise. Don't disappoint."

The more Al poured herself into her work, the more insecure and lost she felt, and the more Dina pushed her. And as she weakened, it seemed to her that Dina got stronger, more flamboyant, as though she fed on her insecurity, like an unnatural creature feeding on its prey, in the thick of the forest, in the dark of night. But she must be mistaken. For Dina had saved her and guided her, tirelessly, doing her best to make her a better artist, a stronger person. It happens in an artist's path that her work dips before it rises. And she would be nothing without Dina.

But Dina became increasingly harsh and degrading. She belittled her and her work, often saying that she made a mistake bringing her to the Factory, that she was talentless.

Al's resolve weakened, her resilience ebbed, and her fingers, always so at ease when holding pencils, were unsteady and unsure. The pages in the sketchbooks stayed empty, and Al's creative drive disappeared. She struggled to explain her process, while Dina looked at her with pity in her eyes, and her own voice became razor-thin, a painful emanation of her soul.

Then Al remembered what the young man said to her and a tide rose inside her. *Adults are really not to be trusted,* she thought. And that tide turned into anger, and that anger into voice. She would show her what she could do, show her she was strong, stronger than her even. But Dina realized she had lost her influence over Al, and she turned away from her.

———————◆◆———————

As new girls and boys came into the Factory, Dina turned her full attention, her passion, and her teachings, to them. And Al saw her for who she truly was—an unhinged predator; and the young, aspiring artists for who they truly were—her next feast. As for the closed-down slaughterhouse, in which the Factory was housed, she saw beneath its veneer: it was neither creative nor a refuge. It was a complex contraption used to crush those who didn't satisfy Dina and her Collective, allowing only a very few to rise, feeding on the hopes and dreams of all those who came looking for understanding, for recognition, for a home. It was what it had always been—a slaughterhouse.

⁕──❦❧──⁕

One day, Dina came into the Factory, and her fury was palpable.

"Traitor, backstabbing little prick, bastard."

The red words flowed unchecked from her mouth as she paced back and forth on the main floor. She headed to the large space beneath an iron landing that served as her office meeting space and made phone calls, and words like "betrayal," "cunt," "ingrate" rose from the uproar of her anger. She looked up, and her eyes landed on Al. She motioned to her to come to her.

"He's your friend, right?"

"Who?"

"That sub-talented young man, Ali."

"He is."

"He's a talentless ingrate. I see that you don't know what I'm talking about. Or he's taught you well."

"I haven't seen Ali since he left."

"Ali did an exhibit in Casablanca."

Al waited. She could tell there was more.

"That exhibit went viral, and he's about to move it around Europe."

"Isn't that what you're trying to do? Get us noticed?"

"No. I try to make you good, better, always better. He called his exhibit *Pharmakon*. That means a poison that's also a remedy. But it also means human sacrifice."

Her hair was aflame.

"In his interviews, he referred to us, the Collective, and

213

our space, the Factory. He said its leader—that's me—feeds on artists and requires human sacrifice. He then said that this exhibit was his attempt, successful, he hopes, to turn the poison he was fed here into a cure. So now I've been getting nonstop calls. And friends in Europe are already pulling back from our projects, taking our funding away, and going to him—he created a collective too, it appears. The little snake. Let's see how long that lasts."

That was the day Al's world changed.

She left the Factory and went to see Ali's exhibit. She looked for him everywhere but couldn't find him. Then a young man, smiling and confident, walked quickly toward her.

"Al! You came. So cool you could make it," he said, and he meant it.

Al stared at him and finally recognized in this solar young man the thin and gaunt artist she knew at the Factory. It wasn't that he was physically changed, but there was a light and a happiness that emanated from him that hadn't been there before.

"Wow. Everything. For everything. This is great. You look great," she said.

"I broke free, Al. I'm not the most talented, maybe, but I found what I needed to say and do, at my level. Nothing big, nothing groundbreaking, no politics or dogma or slogans. Just me. Ali aka Ard," he smiled sheepishly and bowed.

"She said you're trying to destroy her."

"She functions in black and white, in success and failure, great and weak. She sees what she wants to see. For a long time, I was angry at her, ashamed of myself, lost. Then I understood—it doesn't have to be this way, her way. I don't want to think or see the world in binaries. I want to see it in colors, in variety, in the little details that make us good, gentle, or weak, or mean. I'm grateful to her for what she and the Factory taught me, what the other artists there showed me. And I said that, too, in the interview. She didn't hear it. She wants the world to be a toxic place she can burn to the ground. I was angry at first, and hated her for how she made me feel. But she can't help being who she is," he said shrugging his shoulders. "She's perhaps a dying breed, and maybe she knows that, too. I'm grateful to her, but I found my own way, not for glory and impact. A true collective has no fixed hierarchy, it's anti-authoritarian, anarchist even. That's why I created my own collective with friends, and you could join us, if you like. There's always good, if you know how to work with what is."

"Pharmakon."

He nodded, and they both smiled.

"I may join you one day."

"Trust yourself. Look for good, find beauty anywhere, in the most improbable places. That's where it is. We all have suffering inside us, and have to live with it."

———※○※———

But Al never saw Ali again. She would find out later, from Jeanne, after all came to pass, that he had disappeared in a place called *l'Enfumoir*—for being blasphemous, for seeking another way of being, for playing with fire and loving a black woman. The woman whose name he called for—*"Jeanne"*— with his dying breath.

———※○※———

Al went home that night, feeling lost and without purpose. The encounter with Ali, as poignant and true as it had been, had only deepened her feelings of insecurity and doubt. How does one embark on such a journey, without a guide, without rules? How do you know which path to choose among the immensity of choices and possibilities? The hope that Ali offered was too vast, too impregnable.

She picked up her phone, called a number she hadn't used in over three months but that she hadn't had the courage to delete, and placed an order. Thirty minutes later, she went downstairs in the dark, in her socks, and opened the back door. She took the plastic bag and paid up.

On her way back up, perpendicular to the corridor that led down into the two bare rooms and bathroom that were the servants' quarters, and through the darkness, she saw two figures. One, smaller, against the wall, and the other, large and familiar, pressed against it.

She stopped and looked.

She looked until the very end, looked until the larger figure moved away, raised his pants and went into the kitchen. She looked until the small figure disappeared down the stairs that led into the servants' quarters and until the large figure came out of the kitchen, a glass of water in one hand and a sandwich in the other.

That was the image that stuck with her: he went into the kitchen and made himself a sandwich. She knew how he made his sandwiches and what he liked in them—white bread, turkey, cheese, tomato, and mustard. He went into the living-room and, despite the late hour, turned on the TV.

⁕

Al went up the stairs. On her way up, she thought she heard a door close, slowly. She hesitated, then walked to her parents' room, saw the lights were on, and knocked on their door.

"Mama?" she said softly, and waited.

She called her again, and this time the lights turned off.

Al waited, never having needed her mother as much, but the lights stayed off. Al tried to say her name again, but no words came out of her mouth. Just an endless, hollow silence.

She went into her room, took out the stash she had just bought, and let herself go. As she closed her eyes, she exhaled a blue-gray smoke, and the long, thin swirl was full of the words that she couldn't speak.

# 21
# Dada Amber

*"Masters come and go. Wives, concubines, children, those cherished and those despised, come and go. Only the slave remains."*

Her grandmother Yacout had told her so all those years ago, almost a century ago surely. But women like Amber have never counted the years the way the unindentured might do. Instead, they had to be able to see, really see and remember, everything. The homes to which they were confined often became their very remembrance. Amber spoke like a master storyteller, even though she was unable to read or write.

Amber had more stories, and versions of stories, than all the people she knew. She knew stories of ancient times, and old times, and more recent times. But they all fit into each other as though they were all one great story. She walked in the distant past of her ancestors, in her own past, and in an alien present that was beyond her control. She still lived in the time of the oral storyteller, a time endless, circular—neither past, nor present, nor future, haunted by timelessness, ghosts, and supernatural beings. For they walk the earth beside us, and only the ones forgotten by time can see them and live alongside them.

But now time had returned. Amber could sense it.

⸎

They had tried to take everything from her, and from those like her. But there was one thing they couldn't take: desire—the want, the craving, the envy. They might dull desire, but it was always there, even under the cruelest of masters.

They say it's evil, to envy, to want. But it's not: they're lying. They want you to stay in your place, to not question the order of the house, to be ashamed and keep your head down. But envy, it's stronger than them, and stronger than yourself, and it's what saves you. It's always there, lurking. It's the light of the slave that is stronger than any misfortune, any humiliation. It's passed on, generation after generation, weakening the chains, lightening the burden. It's life itself, life reminding you that you, too, are human. You deserve too, you can want and have!

⸎

Amber's inner life was a kaleidoscope of wants and yearnings that she learned to control and subdue as one would a wild beast or an unruly child. And she was able to do so because her mind was quick and razor sharp, and her will was indomitable. It was her best-kept secret: inside her warm, heavy body was a mind that instantly mapped human behavior, positions, weaknesses, and desires—even the most hidden, forbidden ones.

Amber saw everything that happened but never revealed what she knew. She had learned to be patient and knew how to use information in due time. Her loyalties were a matter of survival and pragmatism. She used her skills to ensure that the Mesari household, on whom she depended, endured.

Having arrived with Nadine on her wedding day, Amber's mission, as she had been taught by her mother and grandmother, was to side with the one who needed you most, with the one who would protect you to keep you close.

She offered spells, poisons, and talismans to Nadine for her to keep her husband from straying, and if he must stray, from falling in love, and if he must fall in love, from leaving her. "Spells, poisons and talismans are our medicine for men's fickle natures," she'd say to Nadine. "They bring back the stray husband and trap him into submission. It's a war, my child. A war you mustn't lose."

She saw the way the husband looked at Ghalia, and the way the young maid looked at him. *That one has too many gifts not to be ambitious, not to crave more*, she thought, *but she's fighting a losing battle.*

Amber took matters into her own hands. She slipped herbs and powders into Kamal's food, into his coffee, his tea, which numbed him and made him sad and blue. Not that she believed he could ever leave Nadine for a maid. But he could fall in love, and then the balance of power would shift, and she would lose her privileged position. She spoke about Ghalia on the phone as though Ghalia was a girl who went with many men, said she was manipulative and without scruples. And she made sure Kamal overheard her. It had nothing to do with the fact that Amber actually liked Ghalia, and even respected her, and needed her. It was a matter of survival and balance.

He did things to Ghalia that men had done to her mother, to her grandmother. To her. That was the way of the world. Men will always be men. It's unfortunate that the little girl saw them. But the little girl was strong, and Amber knew she would survive. And she did.

It was what he did to her afterwards, that she didn't expect: how he hounded her, harassed her, threw her to the wolves. And she died because of it. The remedy can be the poison. That young woman died because she wanted to keep her child, a child she never chose to have. Amber remembered her own child, and how she didn't keep her or want to, but then shed the only tears she ever would in her life.

Ghalia fought to keep her child. Her sense of honor and duty was higher than that of any man or woman she knew. But it cost Ghalia her life. Amber had chosen another path. And look, she was still here, alive and with a roof over her head. But oh, the loss and sorrow of that woman's young death.

⋯⟐⋯

They were all gone. They all left. Zahra—who now called herself Jeanne, Nadine, and Al. They asked her to come with them; they assured her she would be free, she would be safe, she would be cared for. But she knew what she had to do.

Amber had only a few moons left in her life—that she knew. Soon, she would join her ancestors, and the only part of her that would be remembered was that she was a descendant of slaves, that her masters still called her Dada, and that even her name was one her mother didn't choose for her.

She couldn't change the past, ancient and immediate, but she could change the course of her life. She could tell and live another story. Did it not happen that slaves rose to prominence, that concubines became queens and the shackled became kings, that masters bowed down to their slaves?

⋯⟐⋯

Dada Amber became the mistress of the Mesari house. She dimmed the lights and put heavy curtains on the windows. What good is it to have a house too bright, too white?

There is no one to talk to or to share her memories with, except Al. For, though men continue doing what they have been created to do, rape and plunder, women now speak differently of it. They speak of choice and money and happiness, while Amber's words are filled with ghosts, poisons, and evil beings who hunt you down lest you trick them first. But she knows something they don't: poisons are remedies. Poisons free you and change the course of your destiny as it meanders from darkened cellar to sun-graced bedroom.

Kamal lost all desire to live. They said he was punishing himself for his evil deeds. That may be so, but the herbs she sprinkled on his food, in his coffee and his tea, might have aided him down his path to repentance.

Now, she has a room upstairs where she can rest her old bones. The room is Kamal's and Nadine's dead little boy's room that has remained empty since his death and where only Kamal had ever come in, lying down on the floor and sobbing himself to sleep until daybreak, unbeknownst to all but to Amber.

Whenever Al came to visit, they'd have tea in her room with a window facing the garden, and talk quietly about the little things that bring them both happiness.

She felt the light dim inside her, and she hoped that it would be passed on to another person in need: a young girl married to an old man, a migrant cut loose from her family and who would never love again, a woman opening doors into the unknown, an artist at a loss for inspiration, a little child born in darkness…The light of the slave that is never extinguished.

And so one night, as she lay her head down to rest on the first real bed in her near centennial life, just before falling asleep, Amber decided to choose a name for herself, a name in Arabic.

*El Hourra*...the free one.

# 22
## Of Mothers and Sons

The young boy's marble collection was his favorite thing in the world. It was huge and he knew most of their names by heart. There was the Dragon, green with yellow and orange stripes; the Galaxy, which looked like it held the universe; and the Jellyfish, a smooth white and blue mix. The Unicorn was transparent and looked like it had a yellow and blue eye hanging in the middle of it. The Sunrise had a little sun rising inside. There was the lustered blue, the lustered red, the Cat's Eye, and all the different Stardusts—blue, orange, yellow, red. But his favorite was the large transparent marble that sometimes came with white flecks: the Pearlie. He could hit the smaller marbles with it, and it would even reflect the other marbles.

*Imagine living inside it*, he thought. He could float in a sea of white and stardust, and everyone would watch and admire him but never be able to touch him. And no one would ever ignore or make fun of him again. This was an especially vivid and useful dream when he was trying to shut out his parents' incessant fighting. His biggest fear was that they would take away his collection and he'd have nothing of his own that made him happy.

Kamal Mesari didn't have friends. He didn't know how to play or laugh or even talk with kids his age, except when they played marbles together. The problem was that he'd get angry so easily and even start crying if a game didn't go his way. And soon, the other boys stopped playing with him altogether. "Big crybaby," they'd call after him when he'd suddenly pick up his marbles, put them carefully in their bag and, tears falling freely down his cheeks, run off.

By the age of ten, no one played with marbles at school anyways, and so he was left alone, at home, arranging and rearranging them, from most common to rarest, lightest to darkest, smallest to largest, and, always, his most loved marble, the large transparent stardust, safely tucked behind his bed.

Then on the day of his twelfth birthday, his mother, Radia Ahensal, took his entire collection away from him, even the large transparent stardust. He didn't know how she knew where it was, but his mother always seemed to know everything. His mother was a large, tall woman whom everyone, including her family and even his father, found terrifying.

"Enough with the marbles. You're not a child anymore. Big boys don't play with marbles. It's time to toughen up. I need a man around the house."

*But there's Dad,* he thought, his father, gentle and quiet. But he didn't dare say it.

"I know what you're thinking," she said, always reading his mind. "Your father isn't a man. He's a weak coward. You're the real man—you're an Ahensal. You get your strength from the great plains of the Chaouia, like your uncles and your grandfather. You're from one of the greatest tribal confederacies of the nation. Our people fight till the end. The French know."

She lowered her voice and pointed upwards.

"Even He knows."

Then, her face changed, from proud, haughty woman to gentle, loving mother. She took him in her arms and rocked him close.

"Oh, my son, you're the only one I have. If you don't protect me, who will? Your father hides behind alcohol and women. But you, you're not weak, and sons are put on this earth to protect their mothers, and that's what you must always do. I sacrificed my life and happiness for yours. Even when you're a grown man with a wife of your own, your mother comes first. Heaven lies at the feet of mothers. Your wife will try to take you away from me, they all do. But remember what I'm telling you today and remember also that I'll always love you more than anyone ever will, more than I'll ever love anyone."

Tears welled up in her eyes as Kamal hugged her back. He kissed her hands but didn't know what to say. He couldn't understand his own feelings. Perhaps they were too big and complicated for a young boy to understand, but one day, he would. And one day, he'd be what his mother wished him to be. Just not right away, for he didn't know how, and he did love his father who was always gentle, although more and more absent and distant.

* ———— ❦ ———— *

His mother closed the door behind her.

All that kaleidoscope of color was gone. Those perfect, round, glass treasures he had collected for most of his young life were gone, and Kamal was alone. He had asked his mother for a dog once, but she said only the European children had pets. The marbles of his collection, held securely in his palms or between his finger and thumb, were his only constant and trusted companions.

He thought he'd rather die than face his parents and his classmates the next day.

He pressed the pillow against his face as hard and as long as he could. But he couldn't press it hard or long enough. He must be a coward, just like his father. Kamal cried himself to sleep.

---

The next day, Kamal went to school and tried to keep to himself.

When the school day was over, he walked to the gate and was about to walk home, as he always did, when a sleek, black Mercedes pulled up and stopped in front of him. The window rolled down, and the large, bearded man driving the car motioned to Kamal to get in. It was Bachir Ahensal, his uncle.

His uncle was even bigger and taller than his mother. He looked at Kamal sternly.

"Well, what's this your mother tells me? You play with little glass toys like a girl?"

Kamal stubbornly kept his mouth shut. He never liked his uncle, who was always rough and ate with his mouth open.

His uncle hit him hard on the head.

"It's time you see the world."

His laughter was loud, deep, and slightly insane.

---

The car twisted through streets that Kamal had never seen before. The streets got narrower and dirtier and the buildings on either side older and poorer. Finally, the car stopped in front of a two-story house with a black aluminum door. His uncle told him they were getting out.

They walked up to the house, and his uncle rang the doorbell.

A woman, with heavy makeup and in traditional garb opened the door. Kamal had never seen a woman like her before.

"Back again, Lord Ahensal. Didn't have enough last night?"

"This time, it's not for me. It's for my nephew."

He pointed to Kamal with the cigarette he had just taken out of a silver case.

"First time?"

"His mother wants him to become a man."

"And what does he want?"

"To play with his marbles…"

The woman laughed and told Kamal to follow her.

They went up a steep flight of stairs to a floor with many closed doors through which filtered music and noises Kamal had never heard before. She stopped in front of a door and opened it. He followed her inside.

The room was dark, dirty, and smelled strong. Kamal felt sick. The scent was overpowering, thick and sweet. It was the scent of heavy perfume, imitation incense, and something else that he couldn't quite place but that was overly sweet, overly ripe. He noticed something warm and wet trickling down his leg, and he felt like crying and running away.

The woman stopped him, turned him to face the bed where a figure, whom he hadn't noticed before, reclined.

"Sorry, little man. Your uncle gave his orders. She'll clean you up. Don't worry, it's not that bad, and she's done this before…little men like you. It'll be over before you know it," she chuckled, soft and low. "And you'll never have to worry about being with a woman again."

She turned to the woman on the bed.

"Be good to him. He's the nephew of Lord Ahensal. His uncle wants him to be made a man today."

She closed the door behind her.

———✦———

The woman rose from the bed. She looked tired and old. As she walked toward Kamal, the oversweet, overripe scent became stronger, and Kamal could barely breathe. He understood the smell came from her. He looked around in panic. She took his hand and led him to the sink.

"Come, little boy, let's have you cleaned up first."

She heated the water over a blue gas burner and washed him. Though her gestures were kind and slow, Kamal felt like throwing up. He couldn't stand the way she smelled. It was the scent of fruit when you leave it out for too long and it becomes soft and filled with holes. It was the scent of the dumpster on his street when the garbage men didn't come to pick it up for a week.

It reminded him of the scent of the little kitten who had just been born and who lay asleep against her mother's body. Who was so cute and he wanted to cuddle with her so bad that he took her away and hid her in the cupboard in his room so his mother or father wouldn't find her. He tried to feed her milk and water, but she stopped eating and then she just slept all the time. She soon became hard. He didn't know why he kept her there for days before burying her, crying, under the olive tree in his garden. He wanted to love her and take care of her so badly, and she died. That was the way this woman smelled. Of rot.

He breathed it in, felt it settle inside him, his bones, his muscles, his sinews, his heart. The scent of rot had attached itself to him.

"It'll soon be over and you can tell your mother and your uncle that you're a man now and no one can take that away from you, even if they tried," she said, and there was pity in her raspy voice. "Do what I do, look at the pictures on the wall of all those beautiful cities that I'll never visit but that a rich little boy like you will."

And she proceeded to make him a man, although Kamal was still clearly a boy. She'd have to lie to Lord Ahensal, not that those subtleties were of importance to the likes of him.

Her weight on top of Kamal and the scent she rubbed off on his body and that found its way inside him were too unbearable and too painful. And so, to hide his shame, he did as she instructed him to do and looked at the photographs on the wall.

They were black-and-white photos of streets and monuments in foreign cities with captions underneath each one: The Fountain of Trevi, Rome; London Bridge, London; The Empire State Building, New York; The Eiffel Tower, Paris.

"Well, which one?"

"Which one what?"

"Which city will you go to when you're older? Which city would you like to live in?"

He smiled, a shy, boyish smile.

"Paris."

She nodded. "Why is that?"

He stopped smiling.

"The Eiffel Tower. It's giant, it doesn't look like anything around it and it doesn't care."

The woman, whose name he would never know, shuddered.

"It's cold," she said.

Then she kissed his forehead.

"All right. Do everything you can to get there."

He pushed her away.

"Don't ever touch me again."

And he got dressed and ran out of the room, the rot inside him a constant reminder of his disgust for her, the one who took something away from him without asking him, disgust as well for himself, for being too afraid of his uncle to fight her off. It would not be till many years later, as his mother lay on her deathbed, and he didn't come to kiss her goodbye, that Kamal understood that what his uncle and his mother did to him that day was an evil thing.

Kamal never spoke to anyone about what happened to him that day, nor did he ever shed a tear for his lost marble collection again.

---

Some years later, it was time for him to choose a profession. After a lifetime of being told by his mother that he was her most treasured gift, that he was the greatest, most deserving of his classmates, that others were unworthy of him, jealous and envious of him, despite his mediocre grades, tense relations with other kids, and an inability to form friendships with boys or girls alike, Kamal told his mother he wished to be an architect.

"An architect! What a noble profession. You'd be the first architect in the family. A doctor would have been good, as well. I could have been a doctor, but then you came along, and that was the best thing. Architects are an intelligent choice, especially now with your uncle's and your father's real estate successes."

"I'd like to study in Paris."

"Of course, the most beautiful city in the world. My son, studying architecture in Paris! I can't wait to tell everyone."

But Kamal's grades and recommendations were not good enough to get him into the school he wished to go to. He sat in the living-room with his mother and father.

Radia Ahensal and Hamid Mesari lived separate lives, had separate bedrooms, and barely spoke to one another unless they had to. When they did, it was rarely directly to one another.

"Why don't you stay in Casablanca and study architecture here?" suggested his father. "The school is decent enough, and you're certain to get in."

"No. Paris is the only option," Kamal answered. "Or the United States, but then I'd be too far and that would make me sad."

"This is his ambition for his only son," said his mother scornfully. "He wants you to stay here, go to a school that anyone can get into, instead of going to a city and a school where you'll thrive, where you'll be with people of your caliber."

"That can't happen, Mother."

"No, son, it can't and it won't," she assured him. "We'll find you a school in Paris, without his help…as usual. When has he ever helped with anything around here?"

Hamid sighed and looked at his son.

"My boy, the path you choose today will affect who you are for the rest of your life. Accept that you're not ready to study architecture in Paris. Study here, work hard, prove yourself. Then you'll get in, surely, to the school of your choice, and by your own merit. Don't make the mistakes we have."

"All these years, he's been an absent father," Radia retorted, "letting me raise our son on my own while he was out doing God knows what. It's too late. He doesn't have a say in where you choose to go to school and how."

For the first time in ten years, Hamid turned to Radia and spoke directly to her.

"I haven't taken care of our son because you never let me. You've kidnapped him from me. I never left you because I couldn't leave *him*. Let me be a father to him now, before it's too late for him."

He turned to his son.

"Kamal, stay here, and work hard. Choose a different path for yourself than the one we chose."

His father's words brought to the surface two conflicting forces that underlay Kamal's life: self-aggrandizement and self-doubt. Indeed, the words his mother had whispered in his ears since he was little enforced his sense of superiority. But there was another, timid, small, voice in his head that whispered to him that his mother's words were all lies. That he was worthless and always would be. That he was a fraud; and that's what his father was telling him, too. Stop being a fraud, admit you're not as smart, as worthy, as untouchable as your mother has led you to believe.

At that moment, he hated his father more than he had ever hated anyone in the world, even more than that strange smelling, sad prostitute his uncle had taken him to. He turned to his mother.

"Don't let him ruin this chance for me! You know I deserve it. You know I can do it."

"He will go to Paris, as is his wish, as is his right," his mother instructed his father.

The father stood up, straightened his crisp blue shirt before leaving.

"Then he'll suffer the consequences and you'll have yourself to blame."

"People like us don't suffer consequences," she retorted. "We *make* the rules. It's the others, the weak ones, who pay. He'll do and take as he pleases. That's the way of the lords.

And that's what he needs to prepare to be—a master, not a cog, or a *slave!*"

Her voice rose high to its breaking point, and her words hung in the empty air, unheard and unheeded, for her husband was long gone.

As he watched his father walk away, Kamal felt an immense sadness, and a violent anger.

"Don't cry, there are no tears in this house. You'll go. We'll get you in," his mother said, her voice cold.

---

Those were the first tears Kamal had shed in many years. They were tears of rage and fear. He didn't even cry the day his father died, less than two years later, when he was told the news and was called home from Paris to attend his funeral. He stayed still and quiet for one full day, not certain what to do. Then he packed all his clothes and flew home. He announced then that he would not be returning to France to complete his architecture studies because he had to remain by his mother's side and help her through this difficult time.

And, his mother further explained, her son had to take over his father's real estate business because he was the only one who could. His uncle, Bachir Ahensal, simply nodded, for it would be easier for him to control his vain, twenty-year-old nephew than his fidgety, fearful, late brother-in-law.

But the truth was that Kamal had failed for two years in a row, and the Parisian architecture school his mother and her relations had managed to get him into, had asked him to leave.

Kamal's reputation was built on a lie, which he justified to himself—*They didn't understand what I was trying to do, they're racist, they're jealous. I'm an architect.*

Since he never intended to open a practice, no one could tell for sure whether he was an architect, or not. There may well have been a Moroccan classmate or two at his school who hinted that Kamal had been kicked out of school. But Kamal's family was powerful enough that very few people seemed to care whether in fact he was or was not a real architect. He was relatively wealthy and powerful, and that was enough. As his mother had so keenly prophesized: *"People like us don't suffer consequences."*

---

The Ahensals had made their fortune through the sale and development of their historic Chaouia tribal land in and around Casablanca. Their land became a central asset to the city's rehabilitation of its historic bidonvilles and villages— slums and shantytowns—into modern low-income housing. These sprawling new housing projects dotted the countryside surrounding the city and were more akin to towns than individual building projects.

The land, however, had never been the Ahensals' historic tribal home, as the Ahensals claimed and Kamal discovered during an episode with his very drunk and rowdy uncle Bachir Ahensal.

---

At the end of the failed Casablanca revolts of the early twentieth century, the French administration had rewarded "loyal natives" by giving them the lands of the rebellious Chaoui tribe. The Ahensals were one of these loyal natives that were so rewarded. They had another family name back then, a name they let fall through the cracks of history.

With the country's independence, Kamal's grandfather

signed the new nation's registry. He wrote his name in his fragile handwriting, for, he barely knew how to write. But he had the cunning of a hundred learned men: Mohamed Ahensal.

That is how the land of the defeated Confederation came into the hands of Kamal's maternal grandfather and how his mother's family became the Chaoui Ahensals, historic and legitimate owners of the tribe's lands to the south and the east of the city.

It wasn't until the 1980s that the land brought them their greatest wealth. Following the city's decision to eliminate the slums inside and around the city, their land became prime real estate.

When Kamal joined his uncle in this vast, new enterprise, the construction of high-rises for the poor and the displaced, then in the building of luxurious developments from the land taken from slum-dwellers, he was participating in the cutting off of hundreds of thousands of people's ties and imaginations to their homes, no matter that these homes were made of corrugated iron and dirt floors.

From the little he had learned in architecture school, he knew that the building of peripheral cement high-rises for the poor and the displaced would be a failed project that would create a hopeless, disengaged future for generations to come. As his urbanism teacher told them about the construction of low-income buildings in Casablanca's peripheries:

"You've built the cemeteries of your future, like we did in Paris."

Kamal knew—they all knew, all those who in the eighties and nineties amassed unimaginable riches on the backs of the poor. And no one cared. For when the money came pouring in, millions and millions of dirhams, a frenzy seized the real estate moguls, the new slumlords, the new billionaires who understood one simple fact: greed was insatiable and no amount of wealth could ever appease their thirst. As his mother had said, people like them never pay up. They thrive.

———✦———

By the time he turned thirty, Kamal had it all—except for a wife.

His mother would tell her friends that her son was waiting for the right woman. Good women were rare, and her son needed a woman worthy of him. But Kamal had a terrible secret: he was cursed.

Every time he came near a woman, kissed her, undressed her, her body turned ice cold and she turned her face away. It was his scent. Sickly sweet, like flesh rotting. It was the scent of a deep, impenetrable corruption that he couldn't wash off, no matter how much he showered, how much cologne he poured all over himself, or how many witch doctors he went to see.

"It's a curse. It's in your soul," they said.

"How can I get rid of it?"

And he'd pay them the fees they demanded, without any results, until he stopped going to them, squatting in their crooked rooms and homes.

The scent would only appear when he was conducting particularly sensitive business or when he was with a woman. When it came to business, he became known as "the Devil," and that was good. Fear is a powerful business ally. Though he wasn't as brave or as fearless as people thought he was. His name covered his weakness.

But when it came to being with a woman, it was a curse

that at times forced him to be brutal, or mostly to be with women he paid.

---

Until he met Nadine.

Elegant, thin, blonde, her hair in a high bun. Beautiful mouth, impeccable French, she was perfect. He fell in love with her right away. Their mutual acquaintances introduced them.

"Kamal, the most eligible bachelor in town," a young woman said, "meet Nadine, the newest doctor in town."

Nadine smiled at him and he thought, *How pure and feminine she is. So different from the other women. She makes me believe there is good in the world, good in me.*

She looked him straight in the eyes, and in her eyes he saw a reflection of the best of himself.

She fell in love with him, as well.

Everything was easy and natural with Nadine. They were made for each other. Finally, when he kissed her, she didn't pull away. Instead, she brought him closer to her and put her face in his neck, taking his scent in for what felt like an eternity.

It wasn't long before he told his mother that he intended to marry. Radia Ahensal bit her lower lip until it bled. She quickly brought her embroidered, incense-scented handkerchief to her face, a protection against the evil eye. Her son never made an important decision before consulting with her first, and she believed it would be the same for the woman he would wed. She thought she would be by his side, and they would choose his bride together.

"She's a doctor, mother," he told her, worry creeping into his voice. "Just like you could have been. I think you'll like her."

"I chose you over my studies. That's what a good mother does."

⸻ ❧ ⸻

Kamal brought Nadine to meet his mother. His mother sat in her favorite chair, an end-of-century green brocade armchair. Her white hair was pulled low behind her neck, and her ears, wrists, and fingers were decked in gold and sapphire jewels that gleamed with her every gesture. She wore a simple black velvet kaftan that fell all the way to her feet.

Kamal kissed his mother's hand and gestured for Nadine to do the same. Instead, she smiled and shook her future mother-in-law's hand.

"How do you do, Mrs. Ahensal," she said. "It's an honor to meet you."

Little did Nadine realize that she had, in that one instant, made Radia Ahensal her formidable enemy.

Thin, beautiful, a newly minted doctor, and poor as Job, thought Radia. She had looked into Nadine's past: Educated, certainly. Beautiful, yes if you liked pale beauty. But penniless. Her father was one of those impoverished, wannabe aristocrats who had divorced his first wife, Nadine's mother, had remarried and barely supported his daughter anymore. The mother had raised her on her own and had passed away when Nadine was barely thirteen. Nadine went to live with her father and step-mother, but knew she was an outsider in her father's house.

She was poor and without protection, except for her son's love. And Radia knew her son better than anyone.

Beneath his apparent strength was a bundle of weakness, doubt, and fear. She had made him and knew how to unravel him with a simple tug of the right string. She swore that her daughter-in-law would be forced to deal with her every step of the way, until all the goodness there is between husband and wife, all the hope for peace and love, is perverted and denigrated. Nadine was ready prey for Radia Ahensal.

"Welcome, child," she said.

Kamal and his new bride moved into a renovated house in the gentrifying Palmier neighborhood. Kamal told Nadine that he was the architect responsible for the renovations. Although that claim was false, he had told the acting architect exactly what he wanted, despite the architect's warnings that it would be a hard house to live in. He told him to use white and put glass everywhere, to let light pour in wherever it could.

Kamal's life was all he had ever hoped for.

It wasn't until he found Nadine crying in their bathroom, a few days after they moved into their new home, that Kamal understood that his mother and his wife weren't getting along.

Nadine confided to him that the reason for her tears was his mother's behavior, and Kamal went to speak to his mother.

"You came to my house and looked through my wife's things. You can't do that."

"I can if I want to protect you," she replied. "I don't trust her. She has that old black woman with her, a slave, a witch. She's bewitched you. Look at you, weak and quiet like a little kitten. I hear that even at work you're not a man. I wanted to find the potions she fed you."

"And did you?"

"I did."

She pushed a pungent, brown bag toward him.

"See, smell it. She's drugging you to be her pup."

Her eyes burned with black fire.

"People like us don't suffer consequences. I did it to protect you, son. You're my world. She took your manhood from you. You need to be a man again, and she needs to know her place."

And Radia embraced her son as her voice cracked over the void she was creating.

That night, Kamal didn't go home. Instead, he followed the twisted streets he had known since his late childhood and lost himself in one of them. When he got home the next morning, Nadine went up to him, and tried to kiss him, but slowly moved back.

"There's a scent about you, Kamal. Do you smell it?"

"Is it the smell of the poison you and your witch have been feeding me?"

"What are you talking about? Is this another one of your mother's lies?"

———— ✳ ————

Time passed, and they had a daughter. They named her Alia, like Nadine's late mother. His mother didn't come to see her until forty days after her birth. When she finally came, Radia explained her delayed presence to her son and daughter-in-law this way:

"…Forty days and nights. Once the doors of heaven and hell have closed and there's a chance for this child to live on this earth."

"Mother, you waited forty days to see your grand-daughter."

"When it's a son, I'll pull him out of the womb with my own hands," she answered.

———— ✳ ————

A few years later, when his wife fell pregnant again and the doctor said it was a boy, Kamal was filled with great joy.

"A son—at last, Nadine. Our family can be whole."

He kissed his wife on the forehead, a more tender kiss than he'd given her in many years.

She turned her head away.

"A child you conceived on your own," she said.

"A wife's duty is to her husband, a duty you refuse. Men leave wives who behave as you do."

Kamal left the room.

Nadine had refused herself to him many times in the past. His mother, like a wolf hunting in the woods, instinctively knew what was going on between her daughter-in-law and her son.

"The Quran and our imams tell us that it is a wife's duty to sleep with her husband, just as it is the husband's duty to sleep with his wife."

"What if she's not willing?"

"Consent is not a word that exists between a husband and his wife. Only duty."

And so Kamal, who hadn't shared a bed with his wife for many years, started visiting her again.

"No," she said, "No."

"You can't say no to me. You're my wife," he told her, and he penetrated her.

She stayed cold and quiet beneath him, and his scent—sticky, overly sweet, rotten—became overpowering.

When Nadine developed a fever and their son died at birth, Kamal knew who should bear the guilt.

"The mother's fever is caused by an STD," the doctor told him and Radia.

"And my son's death?" asked Kamal.

"There's a high chance that it's also the cause of the baby's death. In fact," he hesitated, "I'm certain of it."

"It's crucial, Doctor, that you don't reveal the cause of my grandson's death to his mother," said Radia.

"Of course, Madam. We gynecologists often…have to cover up STDs from our patients. We are doctors, yes, but it's also our duty to preserve marriages. What good would it do a wife to know her husband contracted a disease and passed it on to her? Only pain and suffering can come from such a revelation."

Radia nodded.

"That is so, Doctor. That is so."

"Nadine is a doctor, a pediatrician. She'll know we're lying," said Kamal.

And the long-toothed smile appeared on Radia's face.

"Tell her it's an infantile disease. Tell her that it's the measles given to her and to her child by one of her little patients. Tell her that she must quit her practice. Tell her that that's what took our little boy from us."

"Mother, I can't. That will kill her."

"Isn't it what she's been trying to do to you all these years? She's lucky you haven't left her."

"It's a cruel lie."

"Who cares about truth or lies? Who utters them is all that matters. It's the only way to save your honor, son. The doctor will write it down as well. Won't you, Doctor?"

She sensed the doctor's hesitation.

"And an intelligent, ambitious man like yourself, who dreams of having his own clinic, will surely accept a small donation from a grateful patient?"

After the death of his little boy, Kamal's self-hatred deepened and he bore his guilt like a second skin. Guilt and self-hatred made him into a hard, pitiless, unforgiving man. How could he feel any empathy or compassion toward others when his own mother never had any toward him, when his father had been too selfish to save him from her clutches, and had abandoned him to her?

Sometimes, at night, when the household was asleep, he'd slip into the child's room, still intact and perfect, as he wanted it to be kept. He would curl up next to the crib, his arm holding it tightly against him. And then, only then, did he let the sadness appear.

Kamal never again returned to his wife's bedroom. He went looking for his pleasure elsewhere, more than ever before, pleasure which was a brutal, cruel, blinding need. Then Ghalia came to work for them.

———◆———

She was a very beautiful young woman, regal, he thought. To his wife's delicate blondeness, Ghalia's beauty was dark, voluptuous, and sung of ages past, of concubines and harems, of sensuality and submission. She was also kind and intelligent.

She didn't look at him the way his wife did, and she respected the work he did at home, for she was under the impression that he was a recognized architect working in difficult areas of the city.

He saw himself in her eyes, and it was that image of himself that he fell in love with. *She could make me a better person, make me the man I was meant to be,* he thought. She was the first woman to show him true kindness and respect in a long time.

He dreamed of possessing her body like the river possesses the land it runs through, of being made whole and strong again. She would make him into a real man, the one his mother dreamed of.

He started off slow, like they did in the Hollywood movies of the 1950s and the Egyptian ones of the 1960s. A man and a woman, loving each other despite their social and class differences. The woman filled with desire and love, but pure and in need of a teacher. The man, strong and knowledgeable, who would reveal the hidden beauties of love making.

The first time he kissed her, in the shadows of his home office, her mouth melted against his, and she pressed herself against him. Kamal lowered his hands and, after what felt like an eternity, she finally pushed him away.

"No. I can't."

She's coy, he thought. Kamal was beginning to have doubts about her. She's lying to me. There's experience in the way she kissed me, in the ease with which she pressed herself against me. She's like those women I meet who come with me for money, for gifts. What if I'm wrong and she's not pure? What if I'm wrong and she's toying with me?

He let go of her.

A few days later, he kissed her again, with more urgency, and design. She let him, and, at the last minute, she moved away. But there was mockery in her eyes, and her lips curled upwards, cruel. She was teasing him and enjoying it.

He tried again, opened her blouse, pulled down her pants.

"No, no. Don't you understand? I thought it would be different with you. That you weren't like the others, that you wanted something else from me."

"The others? Does that mean you've had other men?

You've been with other men?"

"No, I haven't. That's not what I meant."

"Liar."

"I'm not lying, I just mean you're not the first man to try things with me, and I thought you were different."

"When men try things with a woman, it's because she sends signals that she's that kind of woman. It's because they know what kind of woman she is."

"What kind of woman am I?"

"A woman whom men do things to."

She pushed him back, slapped him, and ran away. He thought he could hear her crying as she ran down the hallway. But that only meant he was right.

※

One night, he was in his office drinking his favorite whiskey and he heard someone moving outside his door, walking toward the kitchen. It was Ghalia.

He followed her and waited for her to leave the kitchen. Then he pushed her against the wall, kissed her, and penetrated her. It was smooth as butter. He was right about her. She didn't say a word, only moved her face away from him, it must be his scent, she could smell it now, though she didn't seem to mind it before.

A few months later, she told him she was pregnant. He told her to get rid of it, that he knew a doctor, that he'd pay for it. But the doctor saw her and said it was too late. She couldn't get rid of it. He told her to give it up, to find another way to get rid of it. He told her he'd give her the money to place the child somewhere, far away from them. She didn't say anything. She didn't take his money. And one morning, she was gone.

He called the only person who could help him, the one person who, despite her old age and her many illnesses, would find the strength and the cunning to fix his troubles.

"Mother, what should I do?"

"Find her, force her to get rid of the child, if it has survived. How do you even know the child is yours? Women like that…does your wife know?"

"No, she doesn't know."

"For now. This tramp will destroy you. Women take advantage of you because they see you as weak. But I'm here to look after you, always. We need to talk to your uncle. He has friends who can resolve the issue. They'll find the answers, they'll help you. They know how to handle situations like these. And they owe us. We let them conduct their business in a spot on our tribal homeland. And we never ask questions. Calm yourself. It's fixed. She'll pay for this."

Kamal shuddered. He had heard of these friends of his uncle who conducted summary justice in their own name. He had heard of their blood-soaked hands and their indifference to pain or remorse. And he also knew that the place where they resolved situations, the infamous *l'Enfumoir*, was on land that belonged to his family.

———

When, in the end, his mother, old and sick, heard all that had transpired and learned that Nadine had left Kamal with Al and the illegitimate child, she came to visit him. She came with a basket full of apples and sweet dates under her arm, and rang the doorbell. It was Amber who answered the door.

"He can't see you now, Madam. He's asleep."

"Let me through, slave. How dare you?"

Amber placed her heavy body between the door and Radia.

"I only follow orders, Madam. Mr. Mesari isn't available at the moment," said Amber, that dangerous gleam in her eyes.

Radia Ahensal, once formidable and terrifying, crouched over and appeared as she had become: old, weak and alone. She put the basket on the ground.

"At least, give him this basket. Tell him it's from me."

Amber pushed the basket with her foot.

"Not this time, Radia Ahensal. You may have won every battle, but I win the war."

—◦—❊◦❊—◦—

Kamal observed the scene from his bedroom window and saw the old woman send his mother away. He never mentioned it, not to Amber, nor to his mother or to any other living soul. Who would understand that a son lets his mother be sent away like a beggar? But when his mother got into her car and Amber closed the door, and all returned to the deadly quiet his house had become, the question he had always wanted to ask his mother burst through his teeth.

*"What is a man? Am I a man, now?"*

—◦—❊◦❊—◦—

A few months later, his mother died. Kamal did not attend the funeral.

# Part V

# 23
## Poison and Cure

*The end of the day*

In the evenening of that one long day, Nadine went back to the house on Saint Barthelemy Street, Noor in her arms. As always, it was painfully bright inside. All the lights were on, and sun poured in through the large windows but without spreading any warmth.

Amber opened the door for her. But she didn't embrace her the way she used to, her heavy frame a cushion against the world. Instead, she just looked at her as though she were a stranger, or someone whose betrayal had shaken her trust.

"Oh, you fool! And with a child in your arms. A boy!"

She bent down to smell him.

"He smells like the earth, he looks like the earth, not like you. You went in deep and saw what shouldn't be seen. Didn't I tell you there were other ways? With a pinch of magic, a prayer to the Almighty, and belief in Dada Amber, you would've gotten rid of your rival, your husband's wandering eyes, all the dangers. You'd be the mistress of it all. But no, look what you've done. You know how he can be mastered, how weak he is, yet you chose not to use my tricks. You've put yourself and your daughter in terrible danger."

"Dada, sometimes I wonder whose side you're on," Nadine sighed.

"The side of God, child, God and his angels, the only righteous side to be on. And God wants a home with a Master at the helm," Amber said.

"And what does God say about the *Master's* children with other women?"

Nadine's ironic words softened into an embarrassed smile as she remembered who Amber was, who her grandmother was, and who her grandfather.

"That was wrong of me. You and I, we never talk about it, and we should, but we share…a history. I never forget that," she apologized.

A strange light appeared in Amber's eyes. It was a light that appeared, from time to time, since she was a child, but mostly when no one was watching, when she was alone with her thoughts, or when words, spoken carelessly or jokingly, ignited feelings she preferred to keep to herself. It was a light that rarely broke through, and it was better that way.

She had a secret name for it, the feeling that seized her from deep within her entrails, akin to an endless roar: the light of the slave. The ignored, despised, belittled anger and rage that had fueled her and her ancestors as they stored up their resilience against servitude; pent-up, ready-to-burst defiance.

"What will you do now, child? If you remain here, you know *he* can't stay," she said, pointing to the child. "Where will you go?"

"You know where I'll go. To the secret you kept for me— our way out, Dada."

Amber shook her head.

"I'm too old and my bones too weary to leave this house, child. This is where I'll remain till my dying day, if God allows."

"But that other house, you know it. It sheltered you. It's a good house."

"That was another time, another Amber. I still have things to do here. And so do you."

"Don't you want to be free of all this?"

"Be what, alone and broke? Away from the comfort of this house?"

"You'd be with me, Dada. You've always known me. You set out once, remember?"

Amber remained silent.

"You and your mother, you followed my grandmother. You left the master's house…"

"What do you know of those times, or my mother? What do you know of the fear, the troubles we had then…"

"Dada, it's the men, the masters, who build these prisons of fear and homelessness."

"You didn't live those times, you don't know. Women aren't any better, they can be crueler, more vicious even, than the men. Don't trust your memories, or your mother's memories. Memories are a den of lies. And I have my own."

Nadine held the older woman's hands in hers. Indeed, what did she know of this woman's life? Though Amber had never been enslaved, and though she had had her salary paid and her days off, how often did she ever leave the house? And where could she go when she took a day off, once every month or couple of months?

"I'm sorry, Dada. I love you. I do. As much as I can love anyone…"

Amber stood still.

"Well, you know where to find me if you change your mind," Nadine finally said.

"If you leave, it will be terrible, for us all. Mark my words. Let me help you stay, win everything back," Amber urged her.

Nadine kissed Amber's rough, calloused hands, her beloved hands. For don't all children love their nannies, sometimes more than their own mothers? And don't they expect that love to be returned, simply and unconstrained? When Nadine was with Amber, she became a child again, trusting and eager to be soothed. And not once, not until this day, did she ever ask herself: does she love me back? Is she free to love? Has she chosen who she can love or did I just assume? Can she love a child who will one day give her orders, when she herself hasn't any children of her own?

"Go, my dear. Talk to that man, if you must. But you will regret this day, mark my words. Dada is never wrong. I'll get some warm milk for that mutt."

And she walked toward the kitchen, her steps slow and quiet.

———

"Mom?"

Nadine turned and saw Al standing at the top of the stairs.

Al came down the stairs and peered at the bundle in her mother's arms, lifting the blanket to look at him.

"Is this him? My little brother?"

Nadine's relief coursed through her.

"Meet Noor."

They looked down at the child.

"He smells like the earth, warm and sweet. How beautiful he is," said Al.

Her mother hugged Al close against her.

"Hearing your voice, nothing else matters."

"We do. We matter. It's only fair, Mom. You lost a little boy because of Dad, and now you get another chance."

"This boy's not mine, Al. He's your father's child. Your father has to own up and decide what's right and what's wrong. The best thing would be for this kid to be with his only living parent."

"Is that what you really think?"

"That's what I'm going to tell him."

Nadine's eyes lit up and Al laughed. How good it was to hear her laugh.

"What do you mean, I lost a little boy because of him?"

"You know, Mama, you just need to remember."

Al only called Nadine *Mama*, the Arabic word, so soft and intimate and good, when she put down her barriers, when she needed her.

"How did you find out? How did you know?"

"It was by chance. I wasn't ready for it…I heard Dad talk to Grandmother. I heard what she told him to do, what to say, what to tell the doctor to do. All the lies. But I was angrier at you than at them for letting him get away with it. For believing him, being so blind. I was sure you knew what happened, but now I'm not so sure."

"Part of you knows, and your body burns and aches," Nadine answered. "And the other part of you refuses to know, and the battle and confusion exhausts you until you can't think or see straight anymore. Forgive me, I was afraid. I was unhappy and I turned away from you. I wasn't a good mother to you and you paid the price. But it's not too late, if you let me."

"Yes, but first, mama, you need to remember. You're a doctor and you were told lies."

"About my little boy…he didn't die because of a child's infectious disease."

"He didn't."

"It was an infectious disease, a sexually transmitted illness," Nadine stated simply, thinking back.

"And your heart has been broken all this time."

"It has, yes."

Nadine breathed in the air and with it her recollections.

The strange, sudden fevers during her pregnancy that lasted until after the birth. The new doctor who only said, "I'll give you the treatment. You'll get better, but the medication won't heal you completely…This disease, once you have it, it's there, in your bloodstream." And the pharmacist to whom she handed the prescription, a mature woman, who simply gave her the pill. But when her back was turned, her aide, a young girl with a blue-and-pink veil, whispered to Nadine, "Try not to be with him anymore, you know?"

She wondered at these people in her memories, these people who shared her own professional field, and how all had lied to her—except for a young pharmacist's aide. How she had let them lie to her.

Finally, she wondered how, all these years, her mind had woven stories, delusions, and creatures to shield her from the facts: that her little boy had died because of a sexually transmissible disease her husband had given her. That her husband, his mother, and a doctor had covered it up. And that Nadine herself had felt driven by her own desire to cover up their crime, and to forget.

"I was a coward. I see that now."

"You were a coward for you and for me. You thought that if you confronted him, then it would be over and I'd be left without a father, without protection or a home."

"Yes, that's what I thought. But perhaps it was an excuse. And then, I...just pushed it out of my mind."

There it was, the image that had haunted Nadine's sleep, her dreams, her waking moments: *a man in the dark, in the corridor, holding his hands over a young woman's face as his body moved against hers. Her body didn't move back against his, it pressed against the wall, trying to become the wall itself, to become stone.*

Nadine looked back at Al again.

"You saw it too. That's why you stopped talking. Because you saw him."

Al shook her head.

"No, my voice shut down because I saw *you*, Mama. I saw you see Dad and Ghalia. And you turned your back on them, and on me, and never did anything. Never mentioned it. You didn't even react the next morning—to him or to her—when he walked in and she had to serve him, after he raped her, in our house."

Nadine remembered that she'd been sitting by the window, unable to sleep. She'd heard a noise coming from below, near the kitchen. She went down the staircase to the hallway, stopped in the darkness of a corner when she saw a man and a woman right in front of her, oblivious of her...

Afterwards, she went back to her room. She heard another shuffle of feet and closed the door. Then Al was knocking on her door, calling for her.

Nadine froze as the full violence of the scene hit her and she realized she had been a broken person, already. That, by closing her door that night, she had failed to protect her own daughter. That by forgetting what she saw, she almost lost her self for good.

"And now..."

"Accept that you saw what you saw that night. What should have happened all those years ago when your baby died, and they told you to quit your practice? What should have happened sixteen months ago when you saw them and I lost my voice? You should have done something. Do something now."

Nadine hugged her daughter, a big, fierce embrace, warm and endless like the waves washing over you, like the first sun after the freeze, like the animal who thought her little one had died and finds her alive and well, having fended for herself, and survived. An embrace full of light, of fire, of life.

"I didn't believe I had it in me to be a mother. But I'll find it in me and make it up to you, if you'll let me."

Al nodded.

"I always knew you weren't happy being a mother. And I thought it was because I wasn't a boy, or that I wasn't like other girls."

"No, that's not it."

Nadine couldn't tell her daughter everything. She couldn't tell her that her life had taken a wrong turn a long time ago, and that perhaps she should never have married, or had children.

She kissed Al on the forehead and went into the living-room, where she knew Kamal was waiting for her.

———❦———

He was sitting at the head of the marble dining table, his back resting comfortably against the blue velvet armchair, his arms square on the table as his fingers played on the phone. He was wearing a turtleneck again. His rash must be back, the scent was unbearable. Doesn't he smell it? He used to be good, once…

He looked up at her and his eyes wavered, slightly, barely, the ice cracking on the surface. What if the ice cracked and broke, melted blue down his cheeks?

She finally saw the brutality and callousness that made up Kamal's life. It was clear to her that, after all these years of make-believe, of playing dress-up and numbing her pain, he had held her down as surely as openly abusive husbands hold down their wives, and she had let him do it, by her passivity and withdrawal.

He spoke first.

"You've taken your time. Hanging out with the riffraff."

"Riffraff? He's a respected journalist, and she's the head of a center for single mothers."

"That journalist isn't as squeaky clean as he makes out to be and that lesbian, well, what can I say? Man haters, all of them."

"If Jamal isn't clean, what are you? What am I?"

"We are a family, a husband and wife, with a child, trying to make it in the world the best we can."

"Two children, it seems."

Kamal took a moment to come up with a reply.

"Why now, Nadine? You've been silent all these years. You've ignored me—us—all these years. So now you're trying to redeem yourself, to deny your role, your responsibility in what happened to us?"

"How am I responsible for your decisions, your affairs, your back dealings?"

"Haven't you benefited from it all? A life of comfort, protection, status, freedom to do as you please? How have you spent your days all these years? Did I once, like many husbands do, withhold any money from you, compare you to other women, blame you for not having another child?"

"…What choice did I have? I played by your rules."

"You could have left."

Nadine shifted uneasily.

"With a young child, take the chance you would remarry,

261

have a son, and forget about her, as your daughter, as your heir?"

"Ah, so you do know the rules. I would have respected you. You would have been the woman I married."

"You would have destroyed me, to show your strength, to hide your humiliation."

They both stared in silence at the emptiness around them. But perhaps the emptiness was the shadow of the great machine of history, relentlessly turning its spikes, its wheels, its algorithms, with no one at the helm, following no rhyme or reason, unstoppable, with no master but itself, and no intent but to exist.

Kamal shook his head, clenched his fists, his muscles showing under his tight shirt.

"You've destroyed this family."

"I'm trying to do what's right, to fix what's wrong."

"That's your big mistake. You always think everything is black or white. You accept no compromise, no weakness. But you don't look at yourself, your own shortcomings. How hard you are with others."

"I've tried not to hurt people."

"You knew what I did. You knew it all—the corruption, the bribery, the bad company. The way our country is run, if you want to have your place at the table, you know there are things that have to be done—tough country, tough choices. The stink, the stink that won't leave me, that's killing me but that I live with because I look everything in the eye, because I'm not a coward. Because," and his voice broke, "I had to learn not to be soft, not to be weak."

"And the affairs, forcing women, taking advantage of your position, your power? Trying to dispose of them, dispose of a child—your child?"

"That got out of hand, it all got out of hand. I couldn't control anything. I was in over my head, from beginning to end. But everything I did, I did for you. For Al, for our family. To keep you safe."

"I saw you that night. You raped Ghalia and now she's dead."

"You believe you saw things. It wasn't what you think. I made mistakes. We may not be the happiest couple, but I'm no rapist, and I don't need to force women into my bed. They fall like flies. Women like power, they respect wealth and domination. We've all been raised in this system, the money and power, the biggest turn-ons."

"That's what you tell yourself. Just keep blaming the victim."

"You don't know what these women are like. They play, they manipulate. They use tricks to make a man lose his mind. Ghalia was smart, cunning, ambitious. She was no victim."

Nadine nodded.

"That's what I thought too at first. That's what they told me you'd say."

"Who's they?"

"The riffraff."

"They don't understand our world, Nadine. It's not that simple," said Kamal.

Nadine ignored him.

"And after all the pain you caused that young woman, you did your best to make her disappear, to give up her child."

"She claimed he was mine. How would I know? She wanted me to help her get rid of it. Didn't I try? My reputation would have been ruined if people found out about the doctor and the request for an abortion. That's a *crime* here, right? But I helped her anyways, and it was too late. Then I told her to give it up.

And she would have. But then, when he was born, she changed her mind. She threatened to tell you, and in fact, that's exactly what she did. With that article she let the journalist write, with her sister sending you the article. She's responsible for the mess we're in. But her death, I never wanted that to happen. I didn't know those men well. They had ties with people I work with, with friends in the police force. They said they would just scare her, you have to believe me, not…"

"Not execute her as she was holding her child—your child—in her arms?"

"Can't be sure it's mine."

"He looks exactly like…"

"Nadine, what, we're some egalitarian society? We just pretend, but our hearts and ways are feudal, archaic, brutal, unforgiving…Look, I want to make it right by you. I'll change my ways. Remember how we used to be, before…before we both lost ourselves. Let's take a second chance at life, at happiness—with Al. We can rebuild everything. Move, leave the country, start again somewhere else."

"My spirit broke when my baby died."

"*Our* little boy, *my* son."

"Is that how you think? Do you even remember what happened?"

Kamal wanted to scratch at his back and legs. The rash had flared again, and it burned and itched. He wanted to scratch at his skin until it peeled off and the rash was gone for good. But he didn't move.

"I do remember, but it was a long time ago. Why does it matter? He's gone," he said.

"Tell me what happened. How you remember it."

"According to the doctor, an infectious disease fatal for the fetus, contracted from one of your young patients. But what's the point of dragging up these details? What do they matter?"

"And that's why you asked me to stop my practice. You said that my being a pediatrician and continuing to work caused me to lose my baby. That's how you remember it?"

"I remember that you had a breakdown, and that you chose not to return to work. And I supported your decision and have taken care of us ever since."

"You're right. I chose to stop my practice, because you asked me to. Because what you were really asking me was to believe you, to believe all the lies you, your mother, and the doctor fed me the day the baby died."

Kamal looked at her and stood very still as the stench rose around and through him.

"I stopped working to believe the lies you fed me. But I wanted to believe, oh how I wanted to believe, that I was to blame, and only me. That it was my doing, not my husband's, who slept around while I was carrying his child and then gave me that fatal germ that made me lose my child—our child. Yes, it's good you remember that today."

"The doctor said it was rubella."

"Measles. The doctor said what you told him to say. Doctors here, especially the male ones, think they have a God-given right to administer cures and truths. They believe it's their duty to lie to save a couple, to save the man in the couple. Their right to hide from the wife the STIs the husband may have contracted, lest she humiliate him, or leave him. Their authority to hide from her the husband's illness, lest she believe they are both responsible, and not just her. Hide from her the fact that the husband has asked the doctor to lie, and have her carry the burden of blame and guilt."

"Nadine, it was a long time ago. It was God's will."

"I believe that was the day your spirit broke as well, the day you stopped believing in anything and made others carry the burden of your self-hatred. And you also hated me for it, for letting you get away with such a lie, such a corruption, for not confronting you."

"It was so long ago."

"If, perhaps, today, you had recalled and recounted the facts as they were, I may have found it in my heart to forgive you, at least to understand you. But you didn't. Because you can't. You can't admit your responsibility. There's no way forward for either of us, together. I believe now there never has been."

---

The door opened, and Al walked in with Noor in her arms.

He was awake, and hungry. His cry was strong, full of need and life. Nadine took him from Al's hands and lifted him up for Kamal to see.

"His name is Noor. He has brown skin, light brown eyes, and brown hair. He's strong, and wants to live."

"We'll find a good home for him, I promise. I'll make sure that wherever he is, he'll be well taken care of."

"He's staying with me," Nadine answered simply.

Kamal's eyes turned cold, like ice, like death itself.

"Be careful, Nadine. Don't toy with me."

"He's staying with me and I'm leaving. And Al is coming with me."

"You can take that bastard child, but Al stays. And expect nothing from me."

"Baba."

Al moved forward.

"All this hatred, all this hurt that you caused others, that you caused yourself and your family. You say you did all this

266

for your family. Then accept who we are, what you brought in, what you let in."

Kamal froze.

"Ghalia is gone. And before dying, she lost everything. Her hopes, her chance at a better life, her dignity. I know you've never forgotten your boy who died. I know his death and the lies, far from making it right, broke your belief in what's right. But here's a chance to save a life, when two others are gone."

Kamal turned to Nadine, the ice in his eyes threatening to break.

"What do you want?"

"That you let us go. Recognize this child as your own. It's the only way for him to have a chance. And I won't ask you for anything ever again."

"No," he said.

The stench coming from Kamal had become unbearable. He pulled up the turtleneck to his nose. He wrapped his arms against his chest in what appeared to be a posture of strength. But in fact, he was pressing his arms hard against his skin to ease the ache and the burning. He felt the rash spreading down his back, across his waist, to his stomach, his torso, his shoulders. Felt it creep up his neck, around his neck, pressing against the small bones right below his chin. He felt a terrible dryness and a profound despair. The anger, the rage, the hatred, they were consuming him, imprisoning him, poisoning him, and he had nowhere left to hide.

"All right. Go, I'll do as you ask. But you will receive nothing from me."

"That's understood, Kamal," Nadine said quietly.

"All I ask is for Al to come see me. She must promise to come."

"I will, Baba," Al answered. "But not because you make me. It's because, despite everything, despite right and wrong, despite all the people you hurt, I pity you. And I remember how you were the only one to understand me when I was a kid, before I grew up. And I love you. Aren't we much more than the lies we make up about ourselves?"

Kamal let out a sigh of relief. Or perhaps it was a sigh calling and hoping for peace, and for a forgiveness that he wasn't prepared to offer himself.

---

The itching in Kamal's body eased up, and the scent all but disappeared, leaving a lingering wretchedness in the air as a reminder, a warning. He stood at the door and watched Nadine, Al, and Noor leave the house forever.

# 24

# The House on Butterfly Street

*Summer*

The house on Butterfly Street had been emptied of occupants for years. Though it hadn't always been a happy house, it was a peaceful house. One could even say, it was a wise house. "Occupant" may not be the right word. It wasn't a house to be occupied. It was one to be opened up, to be held onto, one that allowed you in and shielded you from the world, a refuge. And those who found themselves sheltered inside it were there because they needed to be there.

The new inhabitants, however, yearned for more than a refuge, more than a haven from being misunderstood, from displacement. They wanted vibrancy, renewal, balance. Hopefulness, not just an immutable shelter from the world. And so, they came.

Two women, one older and established, the other young and a foreigner, as different from one another as can be, but who had both one fundamental thing in common: they had left a life behind.

A teenager, whose silence and beautiful soul made you move in closer to catch that rare word when she spoke; and a baby, with golden-brown hair, eyes, and skin, and whose perfection made you believe again.

Another young woman soon moved in with them, still full of anger, missing her sister like mad, but with a head full of dreams, and magic in her hands.

A man often came by to sit with them or work with them; he looked, alternately and simultaneously, like a Casablanca born and bred working-class icon and a tousle-haired intellectual. And a woman, who looked, alternately and simultaneously, like the lead singer of a nineties rock band and a kind and tender nurse, made of iron.

Many others came and went, and the house let them all in, though its walls cracked under the weight of stories told, and the pipes sung and broke under the many uses of water around the house.

The new inhabitants reopened the house and brought in new life. They changed what needed to be changed, but they barely touched the small garden at the back, except for the budding herbs and vegetables that Nadine, Al, and Jeanne had planted.

There was the centennial olive tree, the fig tree, the medlar tree, all fruit trees that grew well in the city and didn't drink of the rare water from the parched earth just for beauty's sake. A garden of fruit trees, herbs, and vegetables that, though modest in their gifts and sometimes a little green, were cherished and beloved. And there was a white, wrought-iron bench under the olive tree for those who wished to sit in the garden and be surrounded by its soft, healing buzzing. It wasn't perfect, nor grand by any means, but it was hers, *theirs*.

Nadine had turned the page on close to twenty years, as if her old life had been over for many years already. She left everything behind, except her antique mirror, which she brought with her. It was fitting, indeed, as the mirror came from this very place, the house on Butterfly Street. And when she hung it in the room that had been her mother's and her grandmother's room, on the wall where it had hung for decades before her, the mirror eased into place, and Nadine could have sworn she heard it sigh in pleasure.

*"Mirror, mirror on the wall,"* she whispered that first day, her usually pale and cold eyes now dark and deep. *"Tell me, have we arrived? Are we home? Are we free?"* The mirror (and her eyes and body didn't lie) lit up, warm and bright, and she could feel its heat ripple through her.

Nadine had reopened her medical practice and set up her office on the house's ground floor. Behind her were the days when work, children, and death were intertwined in a fatal tapestry of lives gone awry. Children and their parents would come in and out all day, and sometimes at night.

Those who could, paid, and those who couldn't, didn't. But, she found, people will always find a way to repay you—a basket of tangerines, a tended garden, a cooked meal, a free car repair, a house never burglarized, beautiful words sprinkled across the city, a smile.

And they had given a child a home, and love, despite the law. There was consolation in that, even a happiness she didn't know existed. And a peace, at least momentarily. Because she fell in love with Noor, and she'd gotten Al back and her work back and a sense of purpose once more, which allowed Nadine to brace for the great insecurities and doubts of their future.

<hr/>

Jeanne lived with her. She assisted Nadine in her practice and had, haltingly and with much doubt at first, enrolled in university, to study marketing and economics as a step toward what she'd once dreamed of studying—engineering, building bridges and roads. And she dreamed of bringing her mother and her younger sisters and brothers to live with her. But she tried to not think about that too much, nor hope for it too furiously, lest the thought take root too firmly in her heart and erase the sun from the horizon.

She helped all those in need that came to this home and never once complained about the work, the low pay, the monotony. Jeanne was now part of a project that aspired to help others, and not just a housekeeper anymore. Ghalia's Senegalese friend Lili often came by to see her and kept trying to coax her into coming to surf with her, kept insisting that the sea and the waves would cleanse and heal her. The people she would meet there would reconcile her with life, with this land, away from prejudice and from hate. But Jeanne hadn't the strength yet. "One day, perhaps, one day I'll come to you and learn this sport of easy souls," she would always answer.

No one knew that Jeanne had followed Nadine there as self-punishment, as the deepest of repentance for past inactions, not as a wish for forgiveness but as a pilgrim, as an act of love for the one she had betrayed. Day after day, she broke a little and mended others a little. It would be a long time—but it would happen—before she could become kind with herself, before she dared forgive herself, and before she could pronounce the name of the only man she had ever cared about: Ali.

At first, Ghalia's younger sister Yasmina came only to visit. Her husband never contacted her again, especially after Nayla threatened to tell the Belgian authorities, and his Belgian family, that he had another wife. So, she eventually moved in, and she used the house on Butterfly Street as a training ground where she could try out on willing volunteers her various hair techniques, dyes, and extensions.

Of course, it would only be temporary; until she had sufficient funds to open her own salon. School wasn't for her. She wasn't brainy like her sister Ghalia, and little good that had done her sister anyways, attracting the dangerous desires of men who didn't understand her, were confused by her, for she didn't fit in their airtight categories and didn't bend the way they had expected. She just wanted to do hair, she said.

Nothing made Yasmina happier than to style hair. Moroccan hair, if you know how to read it, holds in its curls and coils, colors and textures, all the tapestry of the people who have inhabited this land over the centuries: dominating one another, violently, shamefully; intermingling, loving one another, seducing one another, amorously, peacefully.

Kinky, straight, curly, wavy, short, long, jet black, bright red, deep auburn, brown, golden brown, golden, white, gray. Made strong but orange by the repeated use of henna, made soft and full of light by argan oil, thick and heavy by castor oil, scented by jasmine, rose and cedar wood, its spectrum spans the tight-knit hair of its southern, African ancestry and the golden one of its northern, Mediterranean shores. Where else can you find happiness but in Moroccan hair?

———❦———

Jamal and Nayla long grieved Ghalia's execution, which they had been unable to prevent, and were consumed with questions about the roles they had unintentionally played in her death: Jamal by publishing Noor's name in his article, and Nayla by failing to provide Ghalia with safe sanctuary. They raged at the futility of their efforts to make even the smallest changes in the antiquated, unjust laws that punished single mothers and their children, but even more at the difficulty of changing the hearts and minds that still gave such laws their power. Laws whose real purpose was to be sure that women and children don't become full-fledged citizens, and that male domination, lost in fantasies and a deep-seated nostalgia for a time that had never existed, remain intact.

But Nayla and Jamal were people of action. Despite their deep-seated regrets and doubts, they couldn't stay away from their work for too long; they couldn't watch all the pain and injustice, and not pick up their tools. Little by little, they returned to their work, each in their own way.

Nayla went back to her center, working with a vengeance, fighting to save lives with all her might, rejuvenated, ready for battle on all fronts. She often came to the house on Butterfly Street, forging links between her center and Nadine's practice, dreaming of building ecosystems, training centers.

Jamal built his one-bedroom farmhouse on a small plot of land in Benslimane, the lush green countryside outside of Casablanca, with forests and even a lake, a rare occurrence in the dried-up Moroccan earth. As often as a solitary man could, he came to visit the inhabitants of the house on Butterfly Street, his car laden with odd gifts he would find in the countryside markets and with the sweet fruit from his fruit trees and the bitter oil of his olive harvest.

He opened his farmhouse to aspiring journalists and fellow writer comrades, transmitting and exchanging experiences. He wrote page after page of what he called a memoir of struggle against the absurd, but one that he saved up to have published after he was gone.

—————◆◇◆—————

As for Al, though returning to an ordinary teen life was hard, and words often locked themselves back up in her chest, she had accepted that her life would never be a normal one, that her path couldn't be understood by everyone, and that she wouldn't always feel or be okay. She knew that her way of loving and being loved, of being in the world and letting the world trickle through to her, would not be understood by many around her.

She knew she would leave the country as soon as she could, as soon as she was strong enough, to explore the many facets that comprised her and that were still taboo in her land, even though she noticed a loosening, an opening up. But with every reassuring, understanding word came a flood of hatred and misperception; with every cure, its poison; and with every poison, its cure. She longed for a day when change, abruptly, would crack the phial. When the balance between poison and cure would shift, and new ways of being would become possible for girls like her, in countries like hers, where suffocating forces try to crush you, but where you learn, better than anywhere else, to fight back. And just as Ali, her artist friend and Jeanne's true love, had imagined, *pharmakon*—art that heals through its intimate knowledge of poison—would become as indispensable as water or sunlight.

—————◆◇◆—————

Al went to see her father regularly, just as she had promised, but he had changed. From the handsome, impeccably dressed man she had grown up with, he had become thin and sickly. as if he was already an old man. He had difficulty looking others in the eye, constant itches that only he could see, and a perfume bottle to hide rotting scents that only he could smell. The times he spent seeing Al were his only moments of joy, and the quiet happiness her presence brought him reminded her that this man was her father and that, despite everything and everyone, despite his guilt and his remorse, he loved her and she loved him. Al hoped that he would hold on to the regularity of her visits and the kindness she tried to show him. But she also sensed he was disappearing in his guilt and remorse, that he lived his life in the dark. In his blue eyes from which all ice had melted, but also from which all light was extinguished, Al sensed her father's final verdict.

⁕

One year had passed since those few days that changed the lives of the inhabitants of the house on Butterfly Street. That day, exactly a year later, Al woke up to a strange feeling in her stomach and a familiar dryness in her mouth. She called her father on his phone, but he didn't answer. She then called the house phone, and Amber answered.

"He's gone, child. He left this morning. He left an envelope. I think it's for you. I can't read it."

Al and her mom got in the car and drove, for the last time, to the house on Saint Barthelemy Street.

⁕

Amber handed the large envelope to Nadine. Inside it were three notes, a small cloth bag that rattled and clinked, and the infamous, gray family civil status booklet—sole property of the husband and father, and in which a woman, a wife, was listed only as mother to his children.

The first note was addressed to Al.

*To my princess,*

*This past year I owe to you. Without you, without the forgiveness I could read in your eyes, I would have left a long time ago. You're the best daughter a man could wish for, and more than one like me could ever deserve. May my pride be with you when the world sees the talent that is yours, and may my love guide you in the path that lies ahead.*

*Your father*

The second was to Nadine.

*To my wife, who wishes she had never been mine.*

*To my wife I once loved with all my being, but lost to the world's corruption, to my corruption, to the loss that I let you carry on your own.*

*I'm not asking your forgiveness. Just that you remember our love as it once was, as it could have been.*

*In this envelope is money for Amber, to remain in the house as long as she chooses. And the official recognition of Noor as my son, in le livret de famille, with my name and his mother's name.*

*Kamal*

The third one was to Noor.

*To Noor,*

*To the son I'll never know, and who will never know me. A father's protection under the law. Your mother's name and honor reinstated.*

*Ghalia Ait Iddin, who died protecting you, who stood up to cruelty and fear, and left you in the loving hands of Nadine Alam.*
    *Your father, Kamal Mesari*

*A bag of marbles like the ones I owned when I was a child, for you to enjoy when you are old enough. Childhood is the rarest, most precious treasure.*

---

Noor—small, dark, quiet. Shunned and discarded by the laws of men, a child such as he, in a country such as his, there are many, there have been many, as many as the stars in the sky. In ancient times, akin to a changeling, never fully human, upon whom prey society's wrath and fear. A child whose destiny was to be unloved, uncared for, ground by society, and forgotten, a discarded cog in the machine, thrown into the margins.

A child who wasn't conceived in joy, a fruit that should never have come to fruition, perhaps, a misconception, but here he was. Noor Mesari. The son of Ghalia Ait Iddin and Kamal Mesari, raised by Nadine Alam as her own child. A child who carried in his soul and in his body the memory of his mother's stoning as she held him close in her arms, close to her heart, as it became faint and low.

And yet here he was. A child whose existence gave joy to the women in the house on Butterfly Street, hope in the reversal of centennial laws and of the fears holding them in place.

---

Later that day, Nadine and Al sit on the wrought-iron bench in the garden, taking in the garden's soft humming. They watch

Noor play under the Erythrina tree, its fiery orange flowers in full blossom, as the child tries to catch a lizard resting on the tree's brown bark. They sense his need and want, the hunger of his baby teeth, and they are filled with doubt and sadness. But just as night follows day, day will follow night, and that's a comfort to be had.

Noor lies down under the tree and yawns, suddenly tired. And the lizard disappears into a crack in the bark.

# About the Author

Moroccan novelist Mhani Alaoui finds inspiration in her roots and in global themes. She studied and worked in the US for twelve years before returning to her country. An anthropologist by training, her multilayered writing vividly depicts lives from her Arab North African cradle, giving voice to intergenerational aspirations, trials, and legacies, particularly through her women characters. While her story-telling powerfully uncovers history's scars, her ever shifting, compassionate points of view invite readers to imagine and seek a more just and kinder world. In addition to *The House on Butterfly Street*, her previous works include *Dreams of Maryam Tair* and *Aya Dane*. A mother of three, she and her family live in Casablanca.